T0157718

ENCYCLOPEDIA
LIBRARY

ENCYCLOPEDIA
LIBRARY

DARRYL GOPAUL

ENCYCLOPEDIA LIBRARY

iUniverse books may be ordered through booksellers or by contacting:

iUniverse
1663 Liberty Drive
Bloomington, IN 47403
www.iuniverse.com
1-800-Authors (1-800-288-4677)

ISBN: 978-1-5320-8214-6 (sc)
ISBN: 978-1-5320-8215-3 (e)

Library of Congress Control Number: 2019913516

Print information available on the last page.

iUniverse rev. date: 09/30/2019

This book is dedicated to my family and those friends who are my family. My wife, our three daughters, and our grandsons and granddaughters all represent our family clan.

1

CHAPTER

FINAL BIRTHDAY PARTY

"Happy birthday, Dad. Imagine, 93 years young, eh?" Elizabeth stated, smiling at her old dad before his birthday party was about to begin. "Mum would have been glad to live this long to see you complete the twenty-fifth book."

The slightly bent old man, Dr Adams, looked at his still-beautiful daughter, who was now in her mid-fifties. How did she get to be that age so quickly? In his mind's eye and his old, watery brown eyes, he wondered about getting old but, in his case, enjoying the trip. He smiled at his lovely, mature daughter, who had taken over the duties of his late wife, Eve who died five years earlier but had done so for over six decades.

His silent thoughts took over when he neither heard nor saw those around him. *Yes, my wife and I lived in hopes of my books' making some money so we could leave a grand legacy in the form of a foundation, which my daughters and grandchildren could carry on after we had departed. Not that we needed any more riches, for we had all done well in our jobs and invested in good pensions.*

His wife of sixty-five years and he had dreamed of leaving a foundation in theirs and their parents' name which would be a grand gesture to their mums and dads. Any money, with interest, would fund the education for children and aged women and men around the world. They loved the idea that their two daughters would run the foundation and adapt it to the evolving realities of their era.

His elder daughter knew about investment and was very conservative in her judgement, so he knew their nest egg would persevere. Till the day that his wife died, five years ago, he had bought lottery tickets as a backup in case the investment of his writing never paid off.

In a strange way, the writing had paid off, for he had allowed his library of books to be sold to an entrepreneur for a handsome amount on the condition that the purchaser could republish the books under his/her name. His own name on the books would disappear.

His wife had laughed when she heard of the offer of two million US dollars, before she died of old age, just physical deterioration. It was now his turn. His pretty wife, Eve, was the only one he ever loved, and he could never understand why such an intelligent girl had stayed with him for sixty-five years of married life.

Speaking to his daughter, he said, "Elizabeth, I am happy indeed to have reached this age, but you should know that Mum and I had an agreement that when one went, the other would not remain behind for long. You see, daughter, it is time that we meet with your sister and have a frank talk of our business. You have more than an idea of our intentions, but you should all know directly from me what we wanted for you all and for our society, who allowed us to thrive in kindness and safety."

He looked around and thought, *Old folks like us no longer have any friends alive, for they all quietly and unobtrusively slipped into the netherworld.*

"Really, Dad, why would you bring up such a morbid topic on this day?" she whispered to him in the midst of the small number of guests who were slowly entering the back garden of his old house, which was now hers. Her dad had found a new apartment close to where he and her mum had lived for their last years together.

"Well, my dear," he answered, "look around. Who do I know here? Now let us see. Ah! Your sister, my other daughter, and there is my handsome grandson with a new girlfriend. I am proud of that boy." He giggled.

"Now, there is the banker. What is she doing here? You have paid all the bills, haven't you, Liz?" he quietly asked his daughter but really did not care.

"Dad, do not be silly. We have some great news for you. She is here to deliver it personally to you, but you must wait. OK?" She smiled at her old dad.

The old man walked towards the tall, pretty blonde woman holding a glass of red wine. But just before he reached her, he paused to look at the great cedar hedge in the back of the garden and whispered, "My goodness, Eve, if you could only see how our hedge has prospered. It is well trimmed and is well over sixty feet high, eh! Old thing, who would have thought so many years ago, this would one day happen?"

He felt a warm arm slip into his and turned around to see the beautiful gaze of pale blue eyes and a smile revealing strong white teeth, an unlined face, and full lips with red lipstick. Automatically, he returned the gaze and smiled, as his writer's mind whispered the unheard words, *Yes, there is only one thing that survives in this world and over the great expanse of time; it continues to demand our attention, and truly, youth and beauty are inextricably tied together.*

"And you are the new banker who has come to celebrate my birthday. But really, you have come to see if I am truly alive, haven't you?" He smiled and patted her arm.

"Oh really, Dr Adams, you do not mean to be rude to me, do you?" she answered quietly. "Your daughter warned me of your strange sense of humour. I am Sam—short for Samantha," she replied.

Just then, a bold young male interrupted Adams's discourse with the youthful blonde banker. "Emily, this is my granddad," the handsome twenty-one-year-old Archer loudly stated, introducing his girlfriend.

"Hello, Emily," Dr Adams said, introducing himself. "Let me ask you, has this young man tried to have sex with you as of yet?" he asked. Archer broke out laughing.

Emily brazenly answered, "Really, Dr Adams, what a question. In fact, we have quite a healthy physical relationship. What else would you like to know?"

Archer enquired, "Granddad, are you trying to embarrass me again, eh?"

"No, my handsome little man I am just jealous of you for having such a beautiful girlfriend. Enjoy yourselves, kids. Give us a hug, Archer!"

The young man quietly hugged his old granddad hard and whispered in his ear, "I love you, Granddad."

The old man nodded and quietly whispered, "I know, my boy. You are the best thing that happened to Grammy and me in the last twenty-one years. You made us live longer and gave us the opportunity to see you grow up to be a good human being. Love you, grandson." Archer sauntered off, girlfriend in tow, but his eyes were wet.

Then, there was a booming voice as Dr Adams's second daughter, Ellen, and her partner, Troy, took over welcoming folks to the birthday with a microphone. They said they wanted everyone to enjoy their dad's special day. This was an unusual party, for many folks present belonged to the scientific community and were actively employed by one of the many space agencies and research labs in his university town, now an academic city.

Dr Adams was caught by Liz, who took him by the arm to see a middle-aged man with a toothy smile. She introduced him as Ed Gollway. He stuck out his hand and introduced himself. "Hi, Dr Adams. I have brought the microchip with your cerebral patterns copied onto a biochip, as you requested. You should know that the Russian rocket entrepreneur group wanted pay up front, and this was done. When the time comes, they promise to take your package to space station 2. They will propel the capsule into deep space to head through and across the Milky Way."

Old Dr Adams was very pleased with all the preparations his daughter had made in accordance with his wishes. He and his wife had planned this for many years, and in the end, with enough funds accumulated, his wife had told him he should begin planning the execution of his final farewell.

As part of these plans, he had instructed his young physician surgeon to remove and freeze-dry part of his bone marrow. A piece had been taken to a special lab, where the living cells were prepared and placed onto an old-fashioned tissue culture, in which Dr Adams had worked fifty years earlier. This modern freeze-drying process did not kill any of the cells; the procedure was done in triplicate and checked continuously. His test cells were viable after many years in a frozen state.

The surgeon was here at the party with his wife, and when they greeted Dr Adams, there were the usual hugs, for Dr Adams had kept in contact with the medical centres in his town. He was known for his weekly visits to the research labs, where he distributed brochures from his long-time friend's business. His friend no longer ran the business, as he, too, had grown old and had seceded his company in his son. Dr Adams knew that at least once a week, his old friend continued to visit his company, which had moved location closer to his home.

This brochure task kept Dr Adams busy for the better part of eighteen years. During those years, he saw a number of bench-working scientists come and go. They came from all over the world to Canada to learn, and many stayed. His country was stable and remained away from political instabilities.

This task also continued to provide Dr Adams with a small income. The monthly checks continued arriving anonymously to his bank long after he sold off his books and had the money invested by his wife, who invariably stated it was in a "no-risk fund." The A & E Adams Foundation Fund had flourished and had doubled its principal over the years. The blonde banker had come to tell him so, or so he thought. He would hear from her soon.

He looked around at the old garden he had planned, fostered, and cared for with his wife for the better part of sixty years, even when it had become too much for them to handle. Then, they had obtained the best help in that business to ensure their little piece of Eden would thrive. When it was necessary for them to leave, his eldest daughter had taken over the property and was in a position to hire the best gardeners to maintain the garden and the house. Yes, he thought, he was happy indeed, now that this little patch of land would remain in the family's hands for a few more years.

This was not just a home; it was an essential part of their lives, for he and his wife had thrown literally hundreds of functions here over many years. Hundreds of folks had also stayed with them, and it was often described as a hotel with a long list of visitors from around the world.

At supper, his old, watery eyes continued to see the joyous memories of past suppers, for which, in his young days, he had undertaken the major task of barbequing steaks. Later, this had expanded to include fish followed by chicken. He also used the barbeque when he cooked his Indian dishes, allowing the spicy smells and pungent odours to remain outdoors.

His wife had been a master chef of the old school, and in his mind, no one came close to doing a roast like hers. Definitely no one else could do her roasted potatoes placed around the roast, which had caused many to salivate when they came for supper. It was not unusual for guests to call the morning after a supper to ask her how she made her roasted potatoes. Over the years, he had heard her kindly explain how she did it. He bent his head as he recalled the instances and laughed a little to himself.

He remembered saying to her, "You know, sweetie, I have heard you give the details of the recipe for crusty roasted potatoes, but you are a mischievous little cheat."

She would look aghast at him. "What do you mean? I am sure I do not know why you are questioning my sincerity."

He would not let it go, for it was now a game, always with the same outcome. "Oh! The poor suckers will do it exactly as you say, then come back and whisper to you that theirs did not turn out like yours."

There would be great laughter as they happily filled the room with the gaiety of a full retired life. "And you know darn well why they did not turn out the same, you devil," he would say.

"I do not know what you are talking about," Eve would reply in mock innocence.

"You know what, sweetie? It took me a long time to work it out, after watching you for many years, and it was in front of me all the time."

She would again pretend. "What was in front of you all the time, Mr Smarty Pants?" Then, they would break out laughing. "You mean the little glass pot with bacon fat in it?"

"Oh! Yes, just that little item that you left out, eh?"

"Dad, how are you doing? Some more champagne?" asked his cute middle-aged daughter Ellen, interrupting his memories.

"Why not, sweetie? Just a little more, but lean me closer to a chair so I can hold on to it."

"Here you are, Dad. Yes, you have a great group here. I hope you are happy."

"Ellen, I am indeed happy, but I would have been happier if Mum had stayed with me for a few more years. Now, it is time for me to make the final arrangements, and her passing away has given me the jolt I needed to move ahead. You know, El, your mum could not believe that our foundation was so well funded. Now, you and Liz can take over and do some good for the world as independent owners in your own business. It was our greatest wish to leave you both with the freedom to work for yourselves on such worthwhile causes."

Again, his eyes roved the garden as he continued. "Young Archer will have a bright future. Look after him if he will allow you to. I love him still after all these years. You and Troy have brought him up to be a well-adjusted young man, and he will be a credit to society one day. That is all any parent can hope for." He looked at his daughter, whose large brown eyes looked seriously at him.

With her usual happy smile, she quietly said, "Happy birthday, Dad. There is no use trying to get you to change or at least delay your plans for a little longer, is there?"

Dr Adams looked up into the blue sky overhead and replied, "El, we have gone over this for many years, and all the steps have been taken. You know how committed we were, your mum and me. I cannot let her down now that she is not here."

Ellen stood up and walked over to meet a new guest's arrival as her dad quietly sipped his champagne. He could hardly taste anything now; it was just a bubbly drink.

2
CHAPTER

MORE DISCUSSION AND PLANS

Two days later, in the little bedroom that had been converted into a home office fifty years earlier and she had kept for her dad, Liz and Dr Adams met to quietly chat. "Well, Dad, what did you think of your birthday party?" Liz asked her dad as he sat at his old desk with his usual distant look, which she and the family knew well. His old computer was still plugged into the wall.

"You know, Liz, it was wonderful of you and Ellen to go through all that trouble. In a strange way, I had a good time, for memories came flowing back to me. Your mum was there, and she chatted to me most of the time. She is keeping her side of our agreement," he replied.

"Oh, Dad, really? Did you enjoy the gift that the bank manager brought for you and the contracts from Europe? They will be taking all your books and translating them to movies and a personal-history documentary of your era," she stated.

"That is what I do not understand, Liz. The books no longer belong to me but to that rich American to whom I gave all the rights. That included the change of my name on the books to his. Why am I getting all these contracts to sign? I no longer own these books. It was a legal and binding contract. There must be a catch, and you must seek help from our lawyer as soon as possible and sort this out, Liz."

Dr Adams turned away to look out the window; this was all too much for him to deal with. This was where his wife would have taken over the details.

"But Dad, did you not understand that Derek added a codicil after buying the books from you? It said he would continue to send a percentage of all incomes earned from your writing to your foundation. He felt that your's and Mum's foundation had the right idea of sharing with many globally. He does not need any more money, for his billions are enough to support the next four generations of his family even if they go mad spending. There will always be enough," Liz replied.

Old Dr Adams looked up at his daughter and quietly said, "Liz, in all my years, I have learned that no one gives away money for nothing. There is always a hook. I am too old to see through the workings of modern-day charlatans. You must do that with the aid of trusted lawyers."

"And now, you must trust me, for I have indeed had the opinions of our trusted lawyers, and they have all said that the demands of this contract must be guided by Derek, the new owner," Liz firmly stated to her seated father.

"Does that mean he has the right to direct our foundation, Liz?" Dr Adams quietly asked, looking up to his daughter.

"No, Dad that is a completely different legal contract under your name and ours. Derek has nothing to do with the foundation," she replied.

"Well, Liz, if you and El are happy that all is fair and square, then it is all in your hands. Just get me to sign over all the details to you both as soon as possible. I would like to spend the last few weeks planning the details of my great journey." He smiled broadly.

"There are a lot more papers for you to sign off on, so put your mind at ease. I shall have your second breakfast brought up to you now, OK?" She touched her dad's head and left the little office.

Soon, he heard the voice of Martha, his new cook, calling from the old dining room. "Dr Adams, I have the fresh kippers ready on rye toast, and there is hot black coffee. Please do not let it cool down."

He thought, *ha the old biddy's ordering me around as though I was a child or something.* To himself, he smiled and waltzed to the dining room, calling out in his best acting voice, "Ah, Martha, my love! Did I hear the dulcet tones of your voice awakening a passion in me? Where are you, my munchkin, eh?"

Then the cook, in her booming voice, called from the nearby kitchen as she entered with a tray of hot food. "Sit down, Dr Adams. I have no time for such silliness this morning." She pulled out his armchair and allowed him time to settle down. "I will bring the hot buttered toast, just as you like it, now." She bustled out of the room.

Seated, Dr Adams quietly reached over to draw his plate of steaming-hot slices of kippers closer to him. He bent his head, for he loved to smell the smoked fish. When the toast arrived, he took one slice over to his plate and loaded up his fork with fish. Then, he placed the fish onto the edge of the toast, which he cut off, and placed the combination into his mouth.

He closed his eyes and whispered, "Oh, my love! My dearest Eve, it tastes just as good as you made it over the years. It has not changed. Am I not lucky to still be able to eat such great foods from our era, eh! Old thing, you know that I miss you very much."

He had completed eating the two slices of fish and had sipped his hot coffee when Martha returned and smiled. "For a man of your age, you sure have a great appetite. Is there anything else you would like?" she asked happily. Adams looked up into the dark eyes of this middle-aged woman Liz had found, who just wanted to look after an old, professional man. She had passed all the trials of cooking exactly as his wife, Eve, had cooked for both of them over the years.

When Eve's hands had been crippled with arthritis for her last years, he had learned to cook and assisted her with chopping veggies like mushrooms, tomatoes, and avocados as well as opening jars and tins. They had done well, for they had numerous new tools, and many veggies could now be bought already chopped and seasoned just as they liked. Cooking or warming was all they really had to do.

On mornings, it now took him longer to get out of bed and shower or bathe in the new watersheds in the fancy new apartments. But after that, his daughter could pick him up and have the wonderful Martha cook what he desired in his old home. However, he loved to go back to his own apartment at the end of the day.

Right after he finished eating and made his way to the bathroom to wash out his mouth, he gargled with the new bottle of mouthwash. He dried his old, brown, veined hands on the clean towels and was coming out when he heard Liz say, "Hello, Dad. I need you in the office to do some work."

"Bring the remaining papers all along, sweetie." He smiled at his daughter. It seemed like a good time to spend with his daughter, who was party to all plans between his wife and himself. It was time for him to execute the final tasks that they had planned for many years. He was excited, for he had it planned that his favourite physician would give him the final injection on an evening when he was alone in bed. Having one's life taken away by injection was now legal in his province. Then, it was up to his daughters to execute the final stages of this magnificiently defined plan in disposing his ashes.

Liz handed him the papers as he looked up and smiled, for he noticed her eyes were wet. "Weep not for me, my pretty girl. I have had the love of my life, and I no longer wish to live without her. You have all done well. We have travelled together and seen a great part of this little planet. We have eaten the best that our planet could offer. Your mother and I were lucky to live on this lovely blue planet far longer than many. But now, I wish to travel further into and through the deep cosmos. Mum and I believed that if we went together, it would mean probably billions of years together, and that is one dream that no one should try to stop us enjoying." He patted his daughter's hands.

He looked at the foundation papers and the amount that was present at the bottom of a page. "Liz, this cannot be correct. Are there really eight million dollars in the fund?"

Liz, the banker daughter smiled at her dad. "Yes, Father. After you and Mum sold off the books, she invested in bank stocks, but our new banker went to the big US organizations and convinced Mum to give them the opportunity to grow the funds."

"Where did all that money come from? We went without such funds for most of our lives and never had savings for long."

Liz replied, "The Europeans paid for the rights to make the documentary, but every time it was shown, more money kept coming from retainers in the contract. The same is happening with the movies of that sci-fi series of yours that a group of young movie directors is releasing almost every two months. The money keeps pouring in, and the investors take out the interest and pass it over for reserved no-risk, income-generating funds." She smiled.

"Liz," he asked quietly, "is the rest of the family OK? Is anyone struggling to make ends meet? How is their education? Have they got loans that are bogging them down or debt that is worrying them? Do not answer, for if they are struggling, you know charity begins at home. Promise me that you and El will make sure the family does not go into debt. Second, the foundation is to help, so if there are close individuals in need in this city, make sure you are generous in attending to them. Sorry for being so pedantic."

Liz smiled, for he had already cleared out all the family debts that she knew of, but it still worried him. "I promise, Dad, and so does Ellen. She would insist that we do that anyway. Rest assured that all our family on both Mum's and your sides will be well looked after."

Dr Adams rambled on, but his understanding daughter quietly smiled as he mumbled the old refrain. "The foundation was a dream of your mum's and mine when we had just enough to look after our immediate family—and, over the years, our friends—but alas, they are all dead." But foremost in his mind were the plans for his final days on Earth. He was now ready to do something he had dreamed about for many years. At first, it had been his private mental meandering or dream, but once he and his Eve had aged past eighty, he spoke to her about it.

She was always quite pragmatic, and one day, she spoke out. "We have always said that we do not wish to live on after one of us has died. I agree with that opinion now that we are in our mid-nineties. We now have the freedom to seek release in our aged state as the quality of life has disappeared at least for me. It is time to prepare, as we have always done, for our own end. I agree, should you leave me, I will seek our colleague and friend to give me the injection. This body cannot function without the assistance of an army of home professionals and I am totally weak, I do not want to be here any longer."

She continued, "Should we continue to live, we would require assistance with continuous medications and supplements. You will do the same, but I shall leave you to make your arrangements, or I shall tell daughter number one, eh!"

Dr Adams recalled how they both had talked about the legal consequences, least of which were money and property, for they had invested their newfound wealth into the foundation, which their daughters would run. They had already explained to their mature daughters what their wishes were to help society.

They had led very practical lives, dealing with little struggles, including, when required by their daughters, never allowing emotions to get in the way. Their daughters must have inherited their parents' pragmatism, for they remained relatively close as a family even after they heard their parents' plan. When, in their late nineties, they told the daughters of their decision to look at end-of-life termination, the daughters listened, and after some basic discussions, they agreed to play their role. In reality, the girls, now mature women, did not want to see one of their parents wasting away when the other one died. They knew how their aged interactions helped them support each other.

Dr Adams found the best radiologist that used new technology to capture human brain pathways that could be scanned and recorded. He explained that he wanted him to do this for him since none of these technologies were available in his life until now. It was proven that these pathways stored one's memories and experiences in neural patterns. His was well aware that this was an important step as they had lived well pass their expected life span so a recording his cerebral patterns was essential to their plans for traveling the cosmos in pieces.

Dr Adams did not have to explain why he wanted his brain patterns and that of his aged wife and he paid to have this work done for him. These considerations by two scientists involved considerations of an enlightened scientific nature than Dr Adams and his wife understood Both these sensible individuals worked as lab scientists for all of 40 plus years so their discussions was that of trying to be the guinea pigs of the new technologies. One of which was keeping their metal capacities intact.

Stem cells could reproduce many organs but there was not yet enough work done on keeping brain cells or tissues alive in vitro It would have been nice in his own humour should he lose his marbles, these pathways could be implanted in a new brain. The intended theory was based on the loss of an organ, but in this case, it was not yet possible to grow brain cells/tissues using the principles of tissue culture and produce new brain cells.

This was an exciting chapter in this unusual couple's lives, for a brain trust took the best minds in psychiatry, neurology, human molecular biology, and other subjects into consideration. The couple embarked on the project using the latest technologies and powerful resources at hand to make numerous brain scans. NASA and European scientists used these new medical techniques on human volunteers, limited to an elderly contingent. Chinese scientists and a few other closed societies that had indifferent laws and ethics collected a great amount of knowledge that they were sharing with Western scientists.

After two years of intensive research, Eve quietly passed away. Dr Adams was distraught for a day or two, but a strange peacefulness then came over him, and his pleasant demeanour returned. That was when he knew he had to move ahead with the last rites and implement their plans. The birthday party was just the beginning as he went over details on what he was leaving for his daughters to execute sequentially. It took well over seven years for his thorough testing and collecting of materials for his farewell decision.

In private as his two daughters got down to the task of what had to be done after their father's planned death. After all the legal documents had been signed and witnessed by his daughters his focus was to wrap up his scientific details of his body parts their storage and the container designed. The surgeon was at hand to get samples of his bone marrow, a biopsy of his brain cells, the micro-recording chip of his brain, his heart functions, and so on.

The plan was to have these deep-frozen and put with the recorded electroencephalographs on a USB stick or microcell. All were miniaturized and placed into a sealed radiation-resistant capsule of about one foot in length, which the space-engineering and biophysics technologists at NASA specially designed.

Dr Adams had paid for these very expensive pieces in his well-designed plans to contain samples of Eve's and his bone marrow and brain patterns in a capsule. Her cremated ashes had been placed under a tree in the nearby park where they had walked for many years while bringing up a young family. Well into their late teenage years, their children had gone on walks through these gardens that were designed for the blind. His ashes would also be placed around the same tree, where a bench inscribed with their names would also rest.

They had laughed, saying when they came back, they would sit under the tree and have a laugh at folks who may be reading their names. Dr Adams had a strange sense of humour and often said that he would keep an eye on all the family's and friends' activities and, if they did anything untoward, he would quietly blow on their necks. He had said this so many times he could never remember all the people to whom he had made the suggestion as either a threat or a promise.

The cognac was sipped, and the physician asked the family to leave. Dr Adams died peacefully, and his body was sent to be cremated. His ashes were spread under the tree with those of his wife as a local piper played the tune of "Amazing Grace." Only his daughters and one grandson were present.

The daughters asked that no tears be shed, for their parents were happy together. He had repeated many times to his daughters, their father had found the love of his life, and no one else would share his remaining hours. He knew that his Eve was next to him. His books and other publications were to be his memorial left to his family. The wealth they had in their old age was put to good use, and his daughters now had the freedom to do so much more without the burden of looking after aged parents.

3

CHAPTER

THE ROCKET LAUNCH AND SCIENTIFIC MUMBLINGS

Within three days of his cremation, it was a cold night as the daughters watched a courier spaceship take off from the Siberian wilderness. They had travelled on the same military aircraft that was now carrying the capsule with samples of their dead parents.

They had left the Canadian military base, where they heard a recording of all the dreams that their cunning parents had planned so many years ago. After months of discussions between them, they knew they could never change their parents' outlandish requests.

In fact, they had little sway in anything, for Dr Adams had done all the planning down to the hour when the Earth ship would leave the Siberian space centre. He had his legal counsel monitor their plans down to the last minute. In this way, he had taken all control of his final steps from his daughters. This may have seemed a contradiction of their trust and honesty, but in fact, it was justified, for there had to be no press release of this unusual plan to send DNA from Earth beings into outer space.

This defined journey would take their parents across the Milky Way to a site similar to Earth's location on the other side of the stream of stars.

The wise Dr Adams had visited academic astronomers involved in mapping the locations of the many galaxies inside, outside, and around the Milky Way. He had also had numerous discussions on which radio signals had the best chance of coming from a life form more sophisticated and evolved than those on Earth.

Dr Adams had given many lectures in his later life when his books were discovered. He deliberately put forward his belief that there, in fact, was a Garden of Eden, but it was really located on Earth and in the cosmos. When the Creator or God became displeased, he did not destroy Eden but placed it in a dimension close by, where no human could ever see it while alive—only after death. The tenor of these talks suggested that when folks on Earth died, their souls went to Eden. From there, they could see their planet as they had left it, and that, in fact, was the Heaven promised.

Dr Adams was old, and organizations asked him to speak paying a handsome fee to him. This gave him full licence to produce a story for others, mainly of the geriatric population, to whom he spoke. His elder scientists and friends, of which there were still many, laughed, even scoffed at his outlandish postulates. While he enjoyed every minute of his ridiculous speeches, one can only imagine the ridicule thrown at Dr Adams behind closed doors, saying these were the mumblings and ramblings of a senile man.

During his nineties, NASA had completed another international space station, but it was located in deep space between Mars and Jupiter, nearer to Jupiter. This was truly a multinational space station, for the Chinese, Japanese, Indians, and Europeans were all involved. The massive station appeared like a small star, but interestingly, personnel and supplies continuously moved between Earth and this new space station, manned by people of different nationalities. The nations were involved in sending their own spaceships to and from it, carrying astronauts and a myriad of supplies.

The journey took so long that a television station was dedicated to permanently giving the whole planet a visual of where the spaceships were at any given time and what was going on in the space station.

To have continued revenue to support such a costly venture, different wealthy organizations and wealthy individuals were willing to pay to have scientific tasks done under the weightless conditions of space and to have experiments exposed to the unknowns of various radiation types in deep space and the cosmos. Many technical universities were interested in having experiments done for them, while industrial types wanted to search and test biological systems as well as develop new alloys, which could only occur under the weightless conditions of space.

An unimaginable number of requests were made, as experimentation on a deep-space station had massive revenue-generating capability. This ensured the station's longevity as well as the creation and testing of new technologies, products that expanded academic knowledge. For the first time, biologists could focus on an environment other than Earth's, which had limited their expansion and knowledge This led to the development of new types of biology, including a more cosmic one, which began to reveal answers as to why Earth had a biological evolution of carbon-based life forms.

It was now possible for a wealthy couple in their last years to avail themselves of these new technologies. Many earthlings of the day may have thought such exploitation and adventure in the cosmos to be frivolous, even scandalous because of the costs involved while social conditions in many parts of the earth remained in the dark ages.

However, from such research, many cancer patients' tumours were arrested at least for a little while, in space. In many ways, this did use Earth's wealth for personal gain, allowing speculation on the merits of testing in the cosmos to continue.

In some quarters, people thought that such an expensive endeavour was a whim with no benefit to humankind as a whole. Even when the "evil" industrialists utilized the space station for creating innovative products for use on Earth, that was understandable to many. However, sending one's body parts into deep space had no benefit to any other creature on Earth, and doubtfully to the individual and his family.

In response, Dr Adams wrote the following diatribe.

Science in Space Continued: A Diatribe

The cosmos is a massive entity with billions of stars, planets and meteors many of which are composed of nothing more than rocks with no discernible life forms. Since space exploration began many decades ago, it has been known that, statistically, life should exist in the external universe.

Life may not exist as carbon-based beings, like earthlings. Other life forms may be made up of any of the billions of different compounds observed in outer space. NASA and other space-pioneer nations sought life first as microorganisms, which would indicate the presence of water and an atmosphere for microscopic life forms.

The problem with such an outlook was it limited Earth biologists' thinking. One thing is certain: while no life form might fit these cosmic conditions, nucleic acid bases abound in the cosmos. The question in what configuration was left for skilled molecular biologists to speculate.

However, our little planet, in a relatively small solar system, has been adding technological waste, such as spent satellites, micro-landers, and a host of other paraphernalia, to the cosmos. Other beings may be doing the same if they were as evolved as earthlings. All the discarded space-related junk came from Earth's soil, which Mankind had altered to fit his needs. Where there was waste, there would be scavengers. These scavengers may not be the types of biological beings who inhabit waste dumps but rather sophisticated ones similar in principle to Earth's archaeologists.

It would not be an unusual occurrence if a civilized life form from a distant planet were to find our junk while travelling through space one day, which would lead them to us. In this way, if we found such garbage in space, we would set up a mission searching for further evidence to prove other life existed in the cosmos.

One could safely suggest that all life forms have a need to search for like beings. While such an encounter might not be friendly, curiosity would override any pleasantries at first contact. Exploration of the cosmos would not be done just for knowledge's sake, and while one would not discourage such an opinion, one must have the overriding endeavour to find biological life that would remove our loneliness as a species.

Of course, other circumstances might allow for such a risky enterprise, such as a search for some commodity depleted on Earth. This could change the tenor of the search from just exploring the cosmos to remove products not owned by any one civilization. The cosmos has an almost unlimited smorgasbord of all that any life form requires. But it is in human beings' nature to own a resource or at least have access to that resource, depending on how vital it is.

On Earth, there is an unlimited amount of water, which is a basic requirement for Earth life forms. To date, all extra-terrestrial searches have revealed abundant water in different forms on many planets. This makes it an explorable resource in a civilization that has lost its water. Our oceans maintain a large number of life forms, sustaining almost half the world's population. Should such a resource diminish, confrontations over this unowned resource would occur between nations.

Humans did not place the life forms in Earth's oceans; neither do they maintain these stocks that have a parallel evolution to humans. Our climate's cyclical nature allows the land to fertilize the oceans using the planet's rivers. Still, the need for survival would undo what the planet has allowed to naturally occur. Already, there are international laws outlining new ownerships that should encourage better proprietorship.

The fact remains, while the outlined metaphor of fishing and taking vast amounts of life forms out of our oceans, with no responsibility to replace them cannot be a sustainable system. Similarly, should such an in vitro experiment that had been done on planet Earth, be carried out in the cosmos, it is possible that an advanced life form may see their rights to mineral resources as been over exploited by earthlings.

In the same way, deep in outer space billions of light years away, there may be beings who have undertaken a task not dissimilar to what our sports fishermen do on Earth.

4

CHAPTER

ALIEN ENCOUNTER— FISHING IN SPACE

A conversation follows between two biological companions billions of light years in the deep cosmos. "It seems that these cloud nets need to be tightened."

"Why do you think that is necessary? Are you losing any circulating space dust?" came the non-curious reply.

"Well, there appears to be a leak of some kind, for our catches have reduced while our monitors still show a tremendous amount of ultramicroscopic dust travelling through this territory in our part of the cosmos."

A companion replied, "Should we ask the robots to review the workings of the monitors before going any further? They should also be asked to repair any damage to our nets they deem necessary."

"Not a bad idea. But should we use the time to look through the analysis of what we have collected to date?" came the reply.

"That would be worthwhile, after which we should analyse our findings and isolate and categorize the catch according to our policies," replied the companion.

Such was the enterprise of planet Orthus, an old, extremely well-developed, and advanced civilization with a viable sun that kept planets in its solar system in stable orbits. None of these other planets had any recognized life forms on them. Orthus, meanwhile, had living biological life forms that had evolved for many centuries. The Orthusians, as they called themselves, had explored these planets, collecting a wealth of minerals and other materials that enabled their technical development.

Using their now-unlimited supply of compounds, they had ventured farther outside their own solar system into the deep space. After centuries, the leaders of this evolved race had begun to lose faith that they'd find other life forms similar to their own—in particular, life forms that would be compatible with theirs and might exist in smaller solar systems similar to their own. They had ceased travelling farther into the unknown cosmos, where long distances, at speeds not experienced, had begun to seem senseless. In fact, this civilization had become quite self-sufficient, for they had available to them sufficient resources to keep their life forms in a healthy and satisfying phase for several generations.

Instead, the leaders of Orthus focused their population on a luxury that promoted research and knowledge for intrinsic values. Everyone had the opportunity to develop whatever crossed their imagination, and endless resources were made available to support all investigations. They developed their creative skills at all levels of science, sociology, music, art, psychology, astrophysics, and mathematics. They had pushed the boundary in further development more than they could have imagined as a mammalian life form. This truly utopian society had evolved due to great wealth and clever leadership.

A small scientific group that worked in the surrounding outer solar system, at the edge of deep space, had undertaken many tasks. The group's ill-defined purpose was to analyse the collection of cosmic artefacts. The group members did so by observing and studying the movement of asteroids and comets flung in different directions. Huge celestial winds would develop, for reasons still unknown to the scientists. Many continued to study the nuclear explosions away from their solar system. They understood that in the cosmos, explosive forces destroyed and made new nebulae, galaxies, and constellations.

Such was the basis of their fascination that it stimulated continued study. They passed their findings to the planet's higher authority, which catalogued and further developed supporting evidence for all the stuff that passed outside their solar system. With advanced knowledge and increased newer technologies, profound sciences were developed as these scientists tested new theories and made innovations in the vacancy of space.

This race of life forms was so advanced that it created its offspring to encourage further knowledge. In this atmosphere, all theories had a chance of being explored to their limit. All findings were kept in massive in vitro and in vivo libraries, catalogued as living or continuously evolving experiments. In every sense, Orthusians had become, unaware of their achievements, a celestial library of powerful knowledge, was formed that was open to their populations.

From Orthus advanced technology, a documenter robot supplied the following.

Planet Orthus: Flora and Fauna

This massive planet lay in an orbit that allowed large botanical plants and giant trees to grow indefinitely. These botanical miracles, by hypothetical measurements, had no equal on the few planets the Orthusians had found to have botanical life forms. Similarly, their butterflies had wingspans of over six metres, and insects were around one-half to one metre lengthwise. Their birds varied in size, between two and twelve metres; even the fish in the huge oceans were as large as several hundred metres long. The predators that kept the oceans' life forms in balance were several hundred metres in length, but there were smaller ones. The variety of other aquamarine species differed in physiology, morphology, and anatomical details.

Many fishes were edible, but this race had long given up hunting or gathering other life forms as a food source. They used simple botanical species of fruits, bushes, grains, and seeds to satisfy their dietary requirements.

However, on their massive savannahs lived quite exotic quadrupeds, of which one race of white stallions could run as fast as any robotic surface aircraft. Others had shorter legs but huge chest muscles and wings, which allowed them to fly. These mammals were allowed to breed and live free in their safe environments. From time to time, there was cropping to balance the populations, but usually, these extras were used to restart populations on new pastures elsewhere on this massive planet.

In the early days of their evolution, Orthusians used these animals as a labour force, but later on, they tamed them and used many for sport. None of these games for entertainment were in vogue any longer because society had advanced, and ephemeral pleasures had disappeared, replaced by a broadened intelligence.

There were families of flying four-clawed lion-like creatures, and a few were still used as domesticated animals by a select older generation that descended from a gentry background. After generations of breeding this species, it became impossible for them to return to a wild state. They gave their loyalty to their historical owners and remained as needless guards in this modern age. In the old days, if there were a threat, they would spring to their owners' defence, but that ability seemed to have been bred into a subservient trait. There were no crimes or wars between the different races of Orthus. It had taken many hundreds, even thousands, of years to get to this utopic state of civilization.

Similarly, in the olden days of Orthus, the tribes had domesticated a huge pod of sea mammals with the same loyalty effect. Even today, there are remnants of the past, for there are advanced, intelligent aquatic life forms that cling with a strange loyalty to their historical Orthusian masters. This allowed for the study of many of these species through an enquiry, instead of through tracers placed on species. The balance between plants, animals, and insects produced supplements such as a honey necessary to yield hormones within the Orthusian populations.

These supplements were co-developed in a symbiotic physiological relationship from which the base life forms played a part that was just as self-beneficial.

The main life forms were mammalian Orthusians who protected and enriched their flora and fauna. Special areas on this massive planet provided for large prehistoric animals such as the dinosaurs, flying lizards, and huge reptiles to exist. The balance for these primitive meat eaters was again brought under controlled conditions that allowed just the right balance between predator and prey. Study of this planet's flora and fauna allowed for the continual study of all living species in their primitive settings as they evolved.

The environments were, in fact, living laboratories used in the study of their planet's primitive past through the anthropology and archaeology in the planet's evolution. The scientists found that all life forms played a vital role in their own physiology.

Within the huge craters in the landscape where asteroids had struck the planet in its early days, mining revealed rich sources of precious metals and elements, which led to the industrialization and development of an advanced civilization. This included building huge cosmos-travelling spaceships. The mammalian population that ruled Orthus was in an ageing state after travelling as far throughout the cosmos as it wanted to without finding a life form similar to its own. These mammals knew they were alone within one of their biological lifetimes' travel on this side of the huge stream of stars and planets that they referred to as the *lighted cosmic stream*.

However, their cosmic "fishermen" were just one of many innovations that kept certain members of their society interested in all that passed through the outer space of their own solar system. These space workers collected materials or remnants that came from the continual cosmic reorganizations. After a preliminary screening of these artefacts that caught their curiosity, all were sent back to the massive organization of scientific workers for a complete thorough evaluation. After this, these items would be filed away in one of the most elaborate library organizations that any imagination could have devised.

Sections of the educated scientific populations continually used the massive collections for their own development, research, and plain curiosity. All benefits from research endeavours were shared with the collective populations of Orthus.

These massive library collections were stored among other extra-planetary compounds, with their chemical compositions listed and preserved for in vitro access by future scientists. Similarly, the planetary biology faculty studied microscopic life forms, including microbe spores, to their ultimate end. After this, they would be stored under in vivo conditions for others to study.

It took many years, and it was surprising when there was interest by the new generation of Orthusians, who selected microbes for their advanced school projects. Even at their early stage of learning and training, these youthful projects had value, for experts in their fields guided the students. As a result, there was little waste, and with the policy that there was no such thing as wasted results, all information was stored in the great library.

All planetary resources were utilized from storage of knowledge in their natural state, and needless to say, it was a mammoth undertaking. To take on such a challenge, Orthusians had changed their policy after developing their planet to serve all basic hygienic factors required for a comfortable, healthy life. Orthusians enjoyed a stable and healthy understanding that allowed any individual with unusual capability and skills to prosper. It was clear that the whole population evolved a philosophy that lived just for life's curiosity, and knowledge accumulation was part of Orthusians' evolution. They revelled in all knowledge. One of the many documenter robots for the library stated, "In the future, somewhere in the great cosmos, a species of life forms will ask whether this was the end form of their type of evolution. Of course, the corollary must question what benefit it has to the race or to the universe. But philosophically, does empirical knowledge collected just for it requires justification? Does it always need to have value for others, unknown to date, in the hope that a species will require it and find it by a cosmic accident?"

The robots of Orthus were programmed to keep their creators' intent in mind. Future minds would know of planet Orthus and what the successful creators did while they were allowed to thrive in this solar system. The creators had built and placed a survivor's chip in all robots, so when all organic life forms died off, robots would continue their mission of collecting information, analysing and storing the specimens of knowledge they gained. However, they would also continue to search for similar life forms that may exist in the great cosmos. Robots would continue the policy in the absence of Orthusian life forms, proving there were no other life forms in the cosmos, as long as planet Orthus survived.

5

CHAPTER

A FISHERMAN'S TALE

"DDL, no inorganic or organic compounds have been captured in any samples in over half a light year. It is time for us to return to Orthus for a rest. Are you ready to take on this trip?"

TDD replied, "Well, we have travelled farther than we have ever done before, and rather than finding more, we have found fewer. Such is the vastness of the cosmos. It puzzles; there is something that lesser mortals than Orthusians must be missing. There is an unusual emptiness, but I have the feeling that a quiet force or being is looking. Its presence is almost palpable. At least we can document that this part of space outside our solar system is entirely empty except for the usual components that make up dark space. There is nothing to report."

"Yes, DDL. Let us troll the space with finer, ultramicroscopic nets on the way to Orthus."

"To be honest, TDD, this is just going over what our sensors have reported as insignificant debris afloat, unsuitable for any investigation, according to the parameters the head scientists set. I would be happy to just head back to Orthus," replied DDL.

TDD remained quiet before saying, "I hate to say this, but I have an irrational feeling that, as we are out here, maybe it is time for us to do the ultra-screening. We have nothing but time to lose. I believe that we should maximize our efforts before the return trip."

"Well, let us follow your irrational instinct on this one. I will get the robot to launch our microscopic nets. You reset the screening parameters and arrange to do the pickup as we troll along," replied the convivial DDL. They would cover the distance of a half-light year using their unusual speed while they placed themselves into a deep sleep for the journey home. They would wake when they began orbiting Orthus. The robots would awake them from their sleep dispensing and serving a warm drink that would slowly bring back their energy.

Massive fine nets were shot out by large cannons; these nets would cover millions of square metres around their equally large spaceship. This was not an unusual thing to do, and if larger debris came into the nets, the robotic support would enhance the texture of that part of the net so it did not break. Of more importance they would not lose a vital piece of element or compound or even biological material. The backup systems were complete in every aspect, so the cosmic fishermen had little fear of ever losing their catch.

Distant monitors would screen all samples collected, and any difficult bits would be harnessed, placed into sealed containers labelled for distribution back on the planet for workers on unusual findings.

After giving detailed instructions and double-checking the parameters, both DDL and TDD entered their sleeping capsule with confidence they were safe. Any picked-up cargo would be safely collected and stored to be emptied securely in aseptic isolation when they arrived on Orthus.

A Fisherman's Capsule

And so it happened that after a long period, the computer called for the cosmic explorers to wake up. But only DDL came to life. TDD did not wake up. On landing back on Orthus, the spaceship computers reported that only one of the crew had returned alive. In such rare cases, an investigation was immediately launched in search of the cause. This also had significance when the individual was a member of the Orthusian astronautics organization and died while on duty in outer space.

An intense investigation was needed to ensure that the death was a normal or accidental occurrence. This ruled out death by an attack of a life form passing through this section of the universe. Hence, a replacement for that profession was justified, and the authorities in charge of population dynamics sanctioned the in vitro conception of a new-born.

Orthusians' births were carefully monitored and controlled so that overpopulation never became a problem. An ovum of an Orthusian female was taken out of a stock of frozen eggs that were contributed by females. From the time they became fertile, they donated their eggs to storage. This allowed adult females to seamlessly carry on with their profession, similar to males, but they continued to mate for pleasure or when their hormones peaked together.

In the case of TDD, a temporary adult replacement taken from the group of spare individuals would fill in for any emergencies. However, a new individual had to have the genetic characteristics required for that profession. Belonging to such a prestigious organization carried a great responsibility; the replacement would take advantage of enhanced genetic abilities. It followed that genetic profiles were vital to the rebirth of a replacement.

In this society, this type of profession came with highly risk-averse responsibility due to the professionals' standing among their peers. Working in outer space carried great risks, but the leaders of Orthus main concern was the possibility of attack by an infectious agent lurking in the environment close to their quadrant of space. They understood the devastating outcome should their susceptible population become exposed to such a pathogen. Much of the planet's health policies were developed to prevent such a risk posed by an unusual cosmic microbial life form that the Orthusians had never encountered before.

The life sciences of Orthusian society had advanced to such a degree that they could achieve the addition of a new Orthusian in under one light year. The reason for such controlled increases was to enhance need over volume of population. Their biotechnology had improved reproduction to such an extent that a new body could not only be made in tissue cultures but could designed with the required skills during in vivo development.

Strange as it seemed, a transfer of experience and knowledge appeared to have occurred in the new born. In the meantime, while there was no emotional attachment to a colleague's death, the findings of the latest trolling of space had been collected and sent to the designated department.

With all the samples collected on this last trolling, before being sent back to the planet, a select group of investigators immediately began an intensive investigation on the death. Among the space dust and pieces of slag from a planet that had gone nova, they recovered a small, strange metallic cylinder. Its barrel was inscribed in strange calligraphy. It was sent to the ministry that dealt with artefacts of a foreign, cosmic nature because of the significance of a possible intelligence signature.

Investigation

The capsule's exterior was completely sterilized using radiation and handled behind huge glass-enclosed barrier hoods. In these hoods, fresh air from the external atmosphere was forced through filters and into the selected environments. All particulate contaminants were trapped in the filters including aerosols derived from a dampness or fluids handled within the contained hoods. There were also heated rows of high-intensity ultraviolet light that would destroy all organic contaminants that might survive filtration. A second group of air filters then removed ultramicroscopic particles such as viruses or viral particles. This sterilized air was then passed into the external environment and delivered into outer space.

It was the task of the nuclear medicine technologists to scan the capsule outside the filtration hoods and check whether there were lingering viral particles or the presence of biological material. This was followed by intensive scans and X-rays of the capsule's insides. The images from within the capsule that the researchers obtained would then give them an idea as to what kind of studies to undertake. There was the risk that some of the scanners and X-ray machines might damage susceptible material within. However, these images were analysed to determine if the researchers could open the capsule under aseptic, controlled conditions.

The chosen conditions ran the risk of damaging the contents within. Throughout the whole procedure, discussions and hypotheses were continually put forward. After all conflicting suggestions were made, a computer determined the logical next steps. Its detached analysis provided these scientists with the probabilities of the operation's potential next steps. The Orthusians were entranced at finding such an artefact that indicated an intelligent life form. Then, the questions flowed as to how and why it was near their section of space.

They were sure it was not a contaminant from their own past explorations, where their early spaceships and technology prototypes were left to float out into the cosmos due to experimental failures. Indeed, the catastrophes of their early attempts to gain entry into space demanded the loss of lives. They had built many space stations and mineral transport ships, which, when they were no longer of any use, they exploded outside their solar system in deep space.

Lives were lost in taking on travel into the deep reaches of the cosmos. However, these early pioneering sacrifices gave this life form the skill in developing new technologies that provided the ability to leave the planet in safety.

The rewards were the rich resources found on dead planets many centuries ago. This alien capsule's finding renewed interest in the study of the cosmos. Most of all, it awakened the leaders of Orthus to the possibility that advanced life forms might be living close to their planet.

They found drawings of two bipedals, each with a head, a body, and four appendages similar to their own, but they looked physically smaller once the mathematicians learned how to decipher the measurements inscribed on the outside. The naked figures were of two sexes; the physical differences suggested these life forms must have in vivo reproduction, when comparing the broad hips of one and the narrowness of the other.

6

CHAPTER

ORTHUSIAN LEADERSHIP, AWAKEN ...

That there was great Interest one could assume and it was bordering on great apprehension. The following Orthus leaders gathered to hold the first meeting of SHAHLA, the Orthusian council, regarding the capsule's findings.

archaeologist's dream. It arrived just outside our space territory, and one has to ask how long it was out there.

"Have we been discovered after we gave up on finding another life form similar to ours? The capsule has an inscribed message still to be translated, which means the life form has an ability to communicate, and therefore is literate and of great intelligence."

Philosopher:

"Chairman Kha of Orthus, you have lucidly summed up what has happened. You are correct to assume that there may be life forms somewhere in the unending cosmos. Have they been reaching out to any other life forms in the cosmos? Maybe, for simil‑ taken many decades ago, or

Kha (chairman)

SHAHLA (Orthus council rulers)

Members: Philosophers, administrators, social scientists, astro
and astrophysicists, molecular biologists, industrial and
developers, dietary physiologists, and a mathematician. Also i
were, Population-equality workers; Planetary and cosmic deve
Astrophysicists: Technical experts and academic exploration

Leader Kha:

"This is a most unusual finding, a simple capsule
from a fine astro-net trolling on the way to Orthus.
Not academically well-developed cosmic fishermen,
just ordinar̲y̲ ̲c̲o̲s̲mic workers, they have done nothing
̲ ̲ ̲ ̲ ̲ ̲ ̲ ̲ ̲ ̲ ̲ ̲ ̲ ̲ ̲lives to date. One of

spectacular in their exploration ii.
these citizens died bringing this sample of a possible life
form, intelligent enough, somewhere in the billions of
galaxies in the cosmos.

"It must be from a solar system with an evolved life
form that had the imagination to reach out in search of
other living beings in the cosmos. Our astronauts had
travelled far and wide throughout this side of the stream
of stars for millennia and found nothing.

"Our mathematicians have calculated that there must
be at least a hundred million civilizations based on
our long-lived civilization and our solar system with its
biological evolution. Such a small metallic capsule has
been found, and based on our preliminary microanalysis
of the metal, its complicated interior seems to hold an

ar reasons as ours
ly they now have sent out
messages in the hope that some intelligence would heed
their call and respond. Is it our outlook, or maybe our
responsibility, to take up a challenge and try to discover
where these life forms are located?"

Administrator:

"Orthusians, we are not in a position to develop an
armada of search vessels with trained astro-travellers to
visit somewhere that we do not know or to find another
life form that may be more intelligent than us. Is that
my understanding? A decision was made centuries ago
not to search anymore, for there were no life forms near
us. The investment now would be too much, and to
what benefit to Orthus?

"This may be an opportunity for our students to analyse
and seek out information as an academic exercise.

Suppose these are hostile life forms sending out a bait to the gullible; we could be invaded, and we are not prepared for any wars. Just ignore the artefact, and place it in our library. I implore you, leaders."

Social scientist:

"Do we really wish to make contact with a species that has already surpassed our thinking by continuing the search long after we, who had the best in technology and space-crafts, failed in our attempt to find life forms similar to us? Would such a species want to meet with us? They might be much more advanced than Orthusians. If they are, will we be able to meet with them on their terms? Will their intentions be kindly or aggressive?"

Philosopher:

"That would be the cowardly way to look at the chance of finding a species as technically advanced as ourselves or maybe much more so. If they are kindly, then there could be synergism between our species, and that would benefit all. If they are antagonistic, let us travel with a plan on how to cope. Surely, we are not so naive as to lack a plan for either option are we? It would be a far better option to go meet another life form so our lives would not continue in cosmic loneliness and isolation.

"Already, there are rumours of disenchantment by our youthful scientists that we have become staid and mentally lazy, avoiding risk when that was the stimulus for our early growth. We should have a more active outlook for our youth, even if it is just to provide them with a challenge."

Astrophysicist:

"After our detailed preliminary investigation of this capsule, maybe our molecular biologists could use their skills to recreate the species from any mammalian cells that may be present. On the other hand, the species that sent the capsule, which must have travelled billions of light years to find our area, implies being billions of light years away. Was this just an accident and not a deliberate act to find Orthus? Maybe they are no longer around as a species anymore, for their planet could have gone nova. How could we ever find a solar system that we know may no longer exist? We are recreating primitive fears, and that must stop now, Chairman!"

7

CHAPTER

A TEAM INVESTIGATION

Chairman Kha said, "We want our best team of professionals on this project, and a detailed evaluation must begin immediately. I caution all workers no damage must be done to this capsule that we have been fortunate to receive. If there are indeed life forms similar to us, it is our duty to do as much as possible to find out about them—maybe even try to contact them. They took the time and effort to reach out to other life forms in the cosmos. The least we can do is reciprocate with all the resources in our possession.

"Professionals, this is probably the greatest knowledge opportunity ever offered to you and all of Orthus. I have spoken and asked that subcommittees be struck, and full details are to be fed to keep our population aware and updated on all progress daily. Whether this life form is alive or dead, it is in our, as well as all living life forms', interest in this great gift of the cosmos.

"There is only one cosmos in which we all live and evolve. It is our duty as a living entity to seek and find out more of our surrounding solar system. Let the subcommittees select the relevant professionals from our planet's population in this investigation. Administrators, you are to find the resources to undertake this project with the greatest urgency. There must be no shortcut in this endeavour because of economic shortcoming."

With that, the chairman stood up and left the auditorium, leaving no doubt that he was serious in his guidance on this project. It was up to the subcommittees to ensure that the population of planet Orthus followed the findings as the teams of scientists recovered them. The Department of Education would have the details and will answer all queries associated with this little capsule.

Applied Working Committee

As the executive council was dismissed after receiving guidance from the planetary council, one group of the subcommittee called to do pioneering research met secretly. This group included the following members.

- A male elder known as Saunders
- A female molecular scientist named Ana
- A male astrophysicist named Chuck
- A male microbiologist named Ra
- A female cosmologist named Sam
- A female scanning electronuclear physicist named Maga

The meeting room was closed off from any interruptions except for the recorder robots in charge of security. The details of what were discussed could only be shared by this committee close to the chairman, who would be first to have the details before he would share information with anyone else on the planet. This committee so close to the chairman was made up of the finest intellectuals on the planet; many of them were trained in ethics and the history of Orthusians' survival.

Research Beginning with Experimental Design

The venerable elder Saunders stood at the head of the table among this small committee and quietly addressed the members. "I feel that I should state that calm and respect should be used in this investigation. May I have your suggestions on what the experimental design should include?"

Ra, the microbiologist, suggested, "I believe that new scans of the tube's surface should be repeated, focusing mainly on the inscriptions. After these are taken, our committee should come together to try and interpret what they might be. At that time, the best minds should be connected to also render their interpretations using knowledge stored in our great Encyclopaedia planetary library. The best robot statisticians and analysis experts are to be found there."

After a period of silence, Maga raised her hand to speak. "That places a great strain on my techniques and equipment. One must remember that the scanning technology currently available has limitations. We may be able to visualize the inside of the capsule, but I do not know whether electronic scans would damage the capsule's contents. Should magnetic scanning be used then we risk placing undue strain on the integrity of the container? It could spring open, and that would have significant unacceptable consequences. Should there be unanimous consent on this being the first step in the design, my team and I would do our best."

At this interlude, Ana, the molecular scientist, stood up and said, "It is true that our team has been able to bring back a number of our ancient animals based on a few strands of extremely old DNA. These animals are now in our historic parks, and we have been able to maintain a number of these creatures, monitoring them until a few have been able to successfully multiply naturally. This success does not mean that it would be possible for us to do the same with alien genetic material. The DNA of an alien, even an ancient mammalian life form, billions of light years away in another part of the cosmos, would indicate a spiritual being similar to us. What right have we ethically to return such a life form to a reanimated life on our planet?"

She continued quite firmly, "Secondly, I am sure the ethics committees will have to deal with these questions. However, suppose we are fortunate to bring back one alien life form and hold it under the conditions in which it could live. What do we do with one individual? Will it be treated as one of prehistoric animals and be kept in a zoo for our populations to gaze at especially if it is a sentient and intelligent life form."

She paused to let her argument have its effect. "There are too many fall out questions that must be answered before any undertaking at the practical level be even considered. How long do we keep it alive? Will we expose it to other scientific groups' for research? Will we belittle it like a primitive animal and let it be shown to our young ones as another specimen found in our animal zoos? There is little doubt that we may have success at collecting a few cells from the capsule and, by using our current technology, find a medium in which the cells could grow. After that, we may be able to document and measure its physiology and even return a whole specimen of a life form with no life in it. Our scientists will do what we are called on to do, but pure ethics aside, this will be an abomination."

Ana sat down and her head dropped in a melancholy state, unlike this race of Orthusians a sophisticated and intelligent cosmic life forms.

Chuck, the astrophysicist, raised his hand. After getting the nod, he quietly said, "Understanding all the complications that Ana, our molecular scientist, expressed, I feel excitement swell in my breast at meeting a new life form that had found its way to our solar system. Even if our molecular scientists are successfully lucky to recreate this life form, think of the explosion of knowledge, ethics apart. Scientific curiosity and exposure to new knowledge, not of our planet or even of our part of the universe but a part of the cosmos that none of us could ever dream of seeing. That mere fact overwhelms me." Chuck choked with excitement.

He slowly continued, "What laws of physics were used to accomplish this massive undertaking of crossing the unending cosmos just to get here? Of even more fascinating and not mere interest, what laws of physics known to us Orthusians were broken to achieve a flight of several billions of light years across a turbulent cosmos? My team dreamt of going to some part of the cosmos billions of light years away, just to see whether different life forms might exist. This is too precious an opportunity not to exploit it to the maximum. I cannot wait to get our hands on the details of its flight and the direction from whence it came."

A silence settled over the group, which suddenly became aware of this privilege and tremendous responsibility of taking on this seemingly unbelievable project. Then, a voice called for the group's attention as Maga spoke to all as if in a trance:

> "That is the terrible responsibility that is tugging at my sense of duty. In using different scanning systems, I must use radio isotopes to find definition. You should all be aware of my problem. I do not know whether the genetic microscopic nucleic particles would be altered in any way should this methodology be used. It is possible that, taking a facetious outlook, I may inadvertently alter the nucleic acids to bring forth a monster or a microbe with severe killing ability. While one will try to be careful, the fact is that we will be dealing with another possible unknown. Radio isotopes have the ability to cause genetic re-engineering of any cell with non-specific consequences."

Ra, the microbiologist, took in this new information. "There is the possibility that we may cause microscopic organisms to enter into a sporulation phase that could contaminate the life form in the capsule. It would then be impossible to delineate the contamination from the original nucleic acids that may be in the capsule. In spite of our isolation technology skills in following the nucleic formation each step, there is a risk. I follow Maga's argument of laboratory risk, but surely, our ultrafiltration systems would prevent that from happening."

Saunders, the elder, interrupted, saying, "Of course, there will be risk but that is our purpose—to minimize risk. However, I am troubled at the ethics of bringing back a sentient life form, if that is possible, into our environment. One wonders, *Will we bring back a mammalian life form as a vegetable, destroying a clever—even superior—mind and brain in our efforts to learn?* Yes, we need education that will spring forth by having such a noble gift from the cosmos, but at what spiritual cost?"

"Yes, great elder of Orthus; nonetheless, it is our duty to undertake this task for our planet and for a sentient intelligent life form that had already taken the risk to get to us Orthusians. We really have no choice, as I see it," stated Chuck.

"I disagree. We all have a choice, for we can refuse this assignment as being beyond our collective abilities and our personal ethics. Who among us is willing to turn down the greatest professional challenge in our lifetime?" Sam, the quiet cosmologist, stated.

"She had remained silent for a long time, listening to the different opinions expressed by her colleagues. "You all have the right to state the extreme arguments and potential risks involved in this project. From the cosmologist's viewpoint, the biology that we practise here is limited to our species. We have no other comparison to match, so whether we like it or not, we have only a single focus on a very limited biology—that of our planet's evolution. Yes, this statement belittles what we know of biology, but it is a fact for all our sciences, other than that of the astrophysicists, she paused.

Looking directly at her colleagues, "However, they, too, are limited by our brief historic journey through one-billionth of the cosmos or even less that Orthusians travelled several decades ago. Our physics practised to date has massively improved, and while we had limited knowledge and instrumentation at the time of our wandering through the cosmos, we are even better equipped today to undertake such a search should we be called to do so again."

Sam had struck a chord with all the professionals gathered in the room. In fact, there was now even greater apprehension placed on their now-recognized limited ability and technology to do justice for this particle that had arrived from outer space. It was refreshing as all were brought back to a sane, unemotional discussion by Saunders, the elder, who continued in his wise, careful statement.

"What you have stated, dear cosmologist Sam, is quite true. Among our senate elders of Orthus, we have thought about and discussed the varied forms in which life could have originated in different parts of the cosmos. We, on our planet, have based all our biology on carbon-based life forms. That is acceptable since carbon, hydrogen, nitrogen, and nucleic acids are found in abundance throughout the cosmos as we had found out during our cosmic travels. However, we searched with the eyes and intellect of a carbon-based species, looking for species similar to our own, and that, too, for the time being, was an acceptable decision."

"We are life forms of our biology but also of our time of living in the cosmos. While it is good to speculate and to try and predict the future, we really have no perspective of what the future will be. We have no facts that would suggest what could happen with new forces that originate from deep in the cosmos."

The old senator looked up towards the ceiling. "Philosophically speaking, we Orthusians are a species most fortunate to have had little to no diseases or major catastrophes from the cosmos, at least not since our population settled down from a kind evolution. What continues to amaze me is how in the middle of this awesome challenge and excitement clever minds undertook the contradictions posed by that powerful of all enlightened minds - ethics a subject that gives no answers and follows no laws," he paused and looked directly at his audience of scientists and others.

"How wonderful of you all to show such consideration to another living being in the universe. You also know that the being could be that of a religious saint, a cunning savage or be just a benign being with a keen mind for adventure. Being whatever it may be, has to have been clever to have its remains sent out into the universe on the chance of his remains being found."

Chuck raised up his hands and got the nod to speak, "Just because I showed great enthusiasm for this project, it does not mean that I do not respect the Ethics aspect of this major undertaking. I know the difficulty that faces our senate but that is their job. They must show leadership and give guidance to us, as a committee and trust that you will keep us as the major group to do the work. We will disagree with our deductions but you have chosen the best of the applied workers capable of this undertaking. Once we begin this task we must be given full support from all levels of the bureaucracy." Chuck sat down and folded his arms.

The old senator smiled turned away from the podium and left the room.

8

CHAPTER

ANALYSIS OF THOUGHT

"Committee members, I ask that you focus your minds and thoughts on the task before us. Robots, you are to scan all thoughts on the subject, after which you are to collate them in sequence as they affect this task. There must be no editing of any thoughts. All must be kept unadulterated and sent to the senate of elders. They will provide guidance as to what direction we should follow," stated Saunders.

The meeting room darkened as the armchairs slanted to fit each member's back. The members' eyes automatically closed, and from somewhere, the darkness of space entered each mind. All the members had the same experience on a late winter's night as stars and galaxies slowly passed before them. In a deep undertone barely audible to the members, classical music filled the emptiness of space. It was not from Orthus, but it had the desired effect of calming the minds.

The image of a mammal with two upper appendages and two lower ones on which the figure walked filled their minds. It was dressed in white and had a head of white hair, long and flowing. When it turned, each member interpreted its eye and skin colour differently. Suddenly, jumbled words in different languages ancient and new, as well as in different dialects and accents, floated to each member's mind, but they each interpreted what they heard differently.

They had messages, but all were different and entangled, not quite clear enough to be interpreted. Occasionally, the voice whispered as the figure began to become immaterial like a ghost or spirit: *"My children, there is much knowledge within the garden that you have not yet explored. Seek with curiosity and kindness the wonders I have created for you. Much you will learn, but this mortal being came of its own volition to seek. I saw but chose to let it find its own way. If it were destroyed during its journey, so be it."*

The members remained in a deep trance, silent. Elder Saunders whispered under his breath, "This is not possible. This has never happened before. We have never seen such a carbon-based or ephemeral being in our long history. We have never received an answer in our millions of years spent 'mind searching' across hundreds of billions of miles into the cosmos. Why now do I dream of this being in my mind's eye?"

The translucent ephemeral being again spoke, but each heard a different message: *"This is one of my hundreds of billions of living life forms in the cosmos. Through his deep love for his spiritual life, he used his intellect and imagination to formulate such a journey to be reborn. He matches my ..."*

The imaginary being slowly turned like a cloud in the sky, shimmered, and then disappeared. The Orthusians collectively remained in a comatose state as more dreams entered their minds.

In the darkness of the room, the green lights of robots moved with dazzling speed as the brain patterns' activity was transferred to recorders, then forwarded across the planet to another group of elder Orthusians hidden deep in a mountainous cave, away from all distractions. There, lying on couches, the elders sipped warm teas, their eyes closed and heads facing up towards emptiness and darkness.

Aged minds recalled planetary experiences as they relived history. Their minds searched for any and all information related to the task at hand. By doing a detailed information search of the huge libraries, they could cover millions of documents. They instantaneously obtained all the desired information without leaving their caverns. There, the elderly had the opportunity to relive what gave them intellectual and spiritual pleasure.

Without warning, communication within the mountain retreat known by only a few select leaders was totally blocked and non-functioning. All information ceased, and the life-preserving need for continual memories disappeared; nothing came to them. They raised ancient heads to refocus as individuals, then as a collective. The mental force they exuded was so powerful the planet seemed to heave violently, like an underground quake, for an instant. But underground quakes had been subdued hundreds of years earlier. The darkness seemed denser; they became completely disoriented but physically remained on their conscious chairs.

They never really lost concentration, for in old age, the Orthusians let their minds deliberately wander off. Without warning, gentle, barely audible music filled their aged minds, causing profound relaxation and a deep intake of breath. Their torsos adjusted to a more compliant posture as their spiritual minds became comforted.

Robotic mental-pattern messages poured into their minds en masse, making it difficult to differentiate one from the other. As in any collective on this planet, their minds separated and allowed the owners to each seek out the one they understood. Cups were lowered, and silence prevailed as youthful thought patterns came flowing through to the elders. What had occurred many thousands of miles away on the other side of the planet was now communicated to them. They were immediately aware of a message that had come while the subcommittee members were in their comatose state, but they couldn't clearly see the form that the subcommittee members had witnessed, just a shadow in white.

The message was clear, but who or what life form spoke with such gentle authority about the cosmos, as though it was indeed its creator? Every Orthusian knew that the cosmos had no beginning and no end for creatures with a set lifetime. It had always been there, and they were just life forms that came here by a cosmos-caused accident. In truth, they may have been formed from the basic compounds in the eternal darkness of space that had always been present.

Just as they had seen planets and nebulae, they imagined themselves as just another creation. Was this a warning, or had one of their imaginations just crossed its patterns with all in the conference room? It had happened before, when a dominant imagination from the old days crossed another's, which may have been a bit slow, to let its own mind remain in isolation and work for itself.

However, there was a definite message and a lead as to what these members intended to work on. They used the elders in this community as a planetary senior senate to which all subcommittees could forward their plans for review. The senate would sanction them or give guidance as to how the subcommittees could improve their applied plans. Today, they had a more complex set of mental patterns from a select few given a planetary mission on which to work. In fact, this most unusual project could have a far-reaching effect on all Orthusians.

As the old minds settled down from their initial surprise, they found that they all heard the same message. They had little choice, it seemed, but they would have to replay it several times. They now needed time to analyse these transferred thoughts before giving their sanction or suggestions on how to set about implementing the mission as the chairman directed.

The elders responded after many days of cerebral debate in the solitude of their retreat. After a period of profound analysis, they made the following pronouncement.

Part 1

The capsule has to be investigated, there should be no doubt. That it has to be carefully opened is also to be taken as fact. That this may be a communication from an alien being, there is also no doubt. But most important of all is that it may have had a protector from the designer of the cosmos, speculative at this time. This goes against our scientific training and a million years of Orthusian philosophy. From our infancy, our race has never embarked on a spiritual force that would allow us to become a population subservient to a "God". On the other hand, too much has been left to scientific speculation, none of which has been proven or could ever be proven. Why does the cosmos exist? It does, for they have had the opportunity to visit a small part just in an individual's lifetime, so a few have seen it. But when did it begin, and what caused its power to be released?

Part 2

In our later and wiser years, we have an overwhelming feeling that we belong to much more than a planetary race. There is an indestructible part of our being, not physical, which becomes more lucid, yet it evades us. We elders feel—some might even say know—that spiritualism is fact. It has revealed itself fleetingly during our mind searches. It suggests and, in the end, proves to us the need to accept this celestial gift in the form of a small alien capsule.

Proceed with caution using your great technical and scientific skill. Ignore all preconceived laws that you have learned in your profession. However, we stress that you must open your minds to learn as you go step by step. You have our permission to open the spiritual part of your being that follows no laws of Orthus. You are free to enter the unknown; just tell us. No item isolated on this project should be discarded, and there is no such thing as "foolish opinions" in spiritualism.

Encyclopaedic Library

This is the repository of the greatest accumulated planetary facts, our sciences and historical details of how Orthusian society developed and gave each living member the benefits of law and order. Even more memories are stored that include the soft sciences and the psychological changes within our populations as we all evolved. Everyone from social workers to those in the hard sciences recognize that much of the planet's complete population indulges in useful work that benefits every individual. As with advanced societies, more information and facts are stored for use by every member of this collective.

Indeed, even more can be deduced if we carefully analyse the data that have been accumulated, but like with all data, few use the data to any significance. With all our advanced technology, Orthusians have not used their powerful mathematical tool of data analysis and abstraction. This is a major shortcoming in our collective tribes that live peacefully, so we have been waiting for a savant to be born to show the path towards abstraction.

The volume of stored information may have been singled out, but only for relevant and superficial data analysis to solve a specific project. Statistical analysis made the results tidy and presentable to those who ruled our planet. But unknown to many, an ancient individual was given the task as proprietor of the great library but also had access to unlimited resources. That individual was apparently forgotten and left alone, thus allowing her to embark on a project of her own imagination and design.

This was Dia, a female intellectual of unknown age and the librarian who was forgotten by the population until there was a need. In her quiet, unobtrusive way, she had made the library the centre of profound knowledge for several decades. As with all efficient organizations that are on the periphery of the population's use, leadership complacency set in, and over time, the library became institutionalized and forgotten. Dia became an icon based on the analysis of philosophical arguments from the beginning of the planet's accumulation of information and knowledge. She used data analysis to sort out and make deductions, which she referred to as *Testaments of Orthus* (unofficial testaments created by Dia).

Dia's Testaments

1. Orthus is a planet, the largest in our solar system of several lifeless planets that orbit a still relatively young sun in a controlled solar system.
2. As a civilized race evolved, many clans combined so that none was left out of the civilization's evolution. Through discussion and compromise, elected leaders made a population that had great wealth that was shared with every individual in the form of food, the comforts of living, and good medicine.
3. After hundreds of years of knowledge accumulation, the leadership that the population had chosen decided to travel into outer space to seek out compounds needed for its own manufacturing and development.
   a. By entering space outside their solar system, the leaders also looked for life forms similar to their own.
   b. Finding much mineral wealth but no life forms, the leaders deduced that they were the only ones in the cosmos.

4. In the Department of Philosophy, scholars with nothing else to focus on decided that there must be more to their own existence and came up with several hypotheses.

   a. Orthusians evolved like any animal species from a microbe that brought several genetic compounds together. Such microbes could inhabit a liveable habitat such as the intestine and upper-respiratory pathway of an Orthusian mammalian body.

   b. The cosmos had a beginning, but when and why it developed and what was the use of the powerful physical energy, had remained unknown.

   c. A supernatural creator may indeed have deliberately created the cosmos for mammalian populations, such as Orthusians, to use it to learn, develop, and evolve. (This was too controversial for public release.)

   d. What would such a creator want in exchange for giving life pleasures and knowledge? What was its motivation for allowing the cosmos to exist?

Dia recorded many testaments, but this was her subject that languished in the wilderness of intellectual decay. Old, dying Orthusians engaged in little development of a possible spiritual phase. They were born, gained experience, contributed knowledge, and then died. Where did all that intellectual energy disappear to? Was such energy dissipated to be reclaimed by the great cosmos? She knew that her powerful peers should be pondering this discussion, but for some unknown reason, they were afraid to enter such a discussion and to challenge themselves.

They had become too comfortable, and that had led to stagnation of thought. In short, intellectual stagnation neutered them. As a result, with no development, parts of the population could not develop any further. They had fallen into a routine and were subsequently reduced to administering projects through subcommittees. This allowed old Orthusians an opportunity to deliberate on their spiritual side that was stifled from birth.

9

CHAPTER

ICONS ON A CAPSULE

The first microscopic scans revealed the following icon.

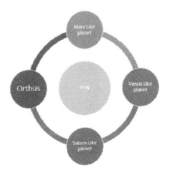

The male sig was o->. The female sig was o+.

Gravestone

There were genetic protein combinations of AT, GC, and U, equal traits and character genetic codes.

"This recovered icon leaves no doubt that this is an alien life form that was showing its solar system. It is a straightforward deduction," Sam, the cosmologist, confidently stated during the committee's first examination. "If there is disagreement, then let me put forward the argument that it is unlikely that scratches by cosmic dust and particles would leave such clear design circles. That is my opinion," she added, staring in disbelief at the clarity of the etching.

Silence continued for some time before Chuck, the astrophysicist, hoarsely whispered, "I agree with that opinion on the circles." The other icons were stared at by all as it became difficult to interpret a tiny circle with a tail on one and a physical distortion on the other.

After many hours, Saunders called for a break from the etchings and asked all to remain in the dark but use the time to ponder. Saunders idly spoke. "That it is part of a communication, there is no doubt, and for the same reasons that Sam expressed earlier of the larger circles. What other information would one of us give in icons if we wanted an alien life form to know of us?"

"Do you think it would want us to know if they are made up of different species?" asked Ra, the microbiologist.

"Why would one wish to provide such a detail?" asked Maga. "It is the first message, and such details should not be necessary," she firmly stated.

"We do not know if that was the first message," responded Chuck. "We do not know if they had sent different messages out from their solar system. In fact, this may be message five or six, not message one."

"That may be the case, but on the other hand, the other icons may not state a race on their plane—rather, differences in sex, if they reproduce like most mammals, as a male and female," retorted Ana. "But that is assuming they reproduce with an ovum and sperm, and not by passing an ovum into a nest for it to hatch as our dinosaurs do."

She looked questioningly at the others in the dark. "There are different ways of reproducing, and we are at risk of discussing only one form."

"Let us leave that bit of discussion for a moment and look at the other icons," asked the calm Elder Saunders. He continued to give direction while stating his own limitations. "The marking is truly alien, and that should be left for our linguists to analyse. But the X or cross has me completely lost, especially when there is a tablet standing on its edge."

Sam, the quiet cosmologist, spoke up. "I have been asking myself what message I would send if I, as an Orthusian, were given the opportunity to send a message into deepest space in the hope of finding another life form of equal intelligence. With the support of superiors, I would first say what my planet and our solar system are like and what we as a species are like. But should the same task be allowed to me as an individual, what message would I send?

"My own biased curiosity would ask different questions. For instance, the first question would be *Are you a friendly or fierce life form?* Next, *Do you have different sexes that allow you to produce the next generation? Would you like some of my genetic material so you can recreate my species on your planet?* Yes, I know what I am saying is outlandish and not logical, but an individual will have different questions. This does not necessarily imply that a whole planet sent a message to seek other life forms. Of course, on our planet, we have a hierarchy that demands that we do not act as individuals. However, there might be planets where individuals have such freedoms to act alone."

She then remained quiet before stating, "Our thinking must go outside all that we know and be open to other forms of governance. There may be civilizations that have evolved with entirely different ways of working together. For example, on our planet, every individual can have nourishment, health, protection, and freedom to work as an individual or within a group. We can have all knowledge and resources that we need to follow our curiosity free of all obligations. A developed society may follow that pattern up until there is a limitation on resources.

"The situation might be that an individual has to earn personal prosperity to get what is necessary from nongovernmental support resources—a sort of ownership of resources that one could sell or exchange for gain as an individual, not a collective. Elder Saunders, would you not sanction that we look outside our current discussion? We still use Orthusian rules, and that appears to limit our outlook."

Elder Saunders stood up, and the lights came on. Still subdued, the participants could see each other lying on their stretched-out cots. He looked down at his feet, then paused. Looking upwards, he said, "The idea that an individual from an advanced life form in a solar system could send a message into deep space had never crossed my mind. Indeed, until it was stated, I would never have considered that a possibility."

He walked to the middle of the room and looked around. "I am going to suggest that we stop all discussions on the icons and proceed to open the vial after examining the in vitro scans, just to clear the air on this type of discussion and speculation, which at this time does not appear to be productive. We should pass these discussions over to the librarian, who I understand is quite adept as a philosophy scholar. I will send all we have been discussing uncensored to her for examination and ask that she use whatever resources she requires to make a logical deduction. There is one condition in that she must get back to us with her interpretation. In this way, we can move forward with our project in a logical order after looking at the scans within the capsule."

The interior scans of the capsule revealed tiny computer chips as found in ancient Orthusian computers, which Chuck, the astrophysicist, immediately spotted. As Elder Saunders viewed the contents, he wondered, *There are hard glass capillaries holding organic matter that appears to be frozen. Next, there are extremely tiny stained, parchment-like dots on a page. It appears that great care was taken in putting these microscopic bits in a set order. This is indeed no accident of a capsule just finding its way after planetary self-destruction. This has all the makings of an alien life form's deliberate act to send delicate matter in the hope that another life form with advanced scientific skills and knowledge would discover it. It came to us! We are the chosen civilization!*

He had to open the discussion on how to proceed, but briefly this time. He would let his subcommittee begin with its observations. His own observation was already scanned from his memory and sent to the senate of elders across the planet in their dark cavern.

Elder Saunders brought his subcommittee to the small meeting room and began a discussion. "Your open comments, please."

Ana was the first to speak. "I have no doubt that the capsule is that of an educated and advanced life form from somewhere in the cosmos. The reason for my strong belief is the well-organized interior of the specimens packed into such a small container. I also believe that we must be very careful when taking the specimens out, as the capsule may have a protective device. This may be in the form of a pathogenic microbe or virus. It has no visible explosive device, which our robots screened out. However, it might have a protective, potentially devastating microbe, to which Orthusians may not have immune protection. There is merit in what I repeat because of the deliberate assemblage of its contents. The meticulous nature of the capsule makes me quite apprehensive, almost frightened."

Ra, the microbiologist, quickly interceded. "Those were my initial thoughts, and I support Ana's comments completely."

Almost immediately, Sam and Chuck jointly agreed and raised their hands, but Chuck explained, "There is no need to be afraid, for we have the option to leave the capsule unopened and place it with our meeting comments and reports as well as those of our senate of elders into our library and museum."

He continued, "However, we were given distinct instructions to undertake one of the most adventurous commissions that our planet has had in centuries, as expressed by our chairman, Kha. Any of us can withdraw from this subcommittee, but as a group, this is a wonderful challenge, and I, for one, will not miss this opportunity, even if it means losing my life doing this task."

Elder Saunders spoke. "Is that a unanimous decision by this committee? Let me see by a show of hands." All hands were raised. "Then let us prepare to handle this capsule under the most stringent conditions of containment and sterilization by as many methods as we can muster. I shall not be the leader, for I am wanted by the senate of elders. I am asking Maga to lead the team. Do you accept?"

"Yes, noble elder, if that is your will," Maga replied.

"Does anyone object to having Maga as the team leader?" he asked. No team members responded and so he thanked them all for their participation and departed immediately.

Upon scanning, Maga, the expert, called the team together and asked if anyone would volunteer to choose safety equipment and have it installed and tested by different committee members. Chuck raised his hand and said, "I will undertake that task but would want Ra and Sam to work with me."

Maga smiled and quickly said, "Approved. Please begin immediately. Should there be any obstacles with regard to obtaining resources, call on me."

As the first group left, Maga called on Ana and quietly stated, "You may have to deal with alien tissue, and probably its nucleic acids and genetic material. We should first find out what risks may be involved."

Ana quickly responded, "I would like to visit our library and speak to Dia. With her assistance, I shall do a complete and thorough search of all literature and review all thought patterns on the subject. After which, I would like to meet privately with Dia on her findings and determinations on this project from her philosophical perspective."

Maga nodded her approval with the added note that the recording robots not be prevented from all discussions.

The teams separated and went about their tasks with the open invitation that, when they were ready to move as a collective, they would gather and have one last session to decide on the next steps to be undertaken.

10
CHAPTER

IN THE BEGINNING

Ana met with her small laboratory team and asked, "Do you think we can repeat our past genetic reconstruction of the dinosaur project using cells from a mammalian being?"

Her chief technologist answered, "Of course, we have all our successfully proven procedures in place, but Ana, is that not illegal?"

"Not anymore, it seems. We must all be cautious, and I want your promise that what I am about to tell you and what you have to do will be held in the strictest confidence. All comments on our work must come from the chairman through the subcommittee," Ana quietly stated.

She then continued, "You are quite correct, it is illegal to perform cell development on citizens of Orthus, but the law might allow us to do it on alien life forms; at least that is what was said to me today."

The chief technologist responded, "Of course, we shall do what you ask in this laboratory. But surely, what is good for Orthusians should also be good for alien life forms, especially if they are similar to us? Should that not be so?"

Ana looked at her quiet group of loyal lab scientists, devoted to the science of molecular biology and who had been working as a team for many years. They had a familiarity among them, which she encouraged. Looking directly at them all, she stated, "You may be correct. At least the principle should be the same, but an ethical exception in this instance has become vital. While I encourage all of you to give your honest opinion, rest assured that the fact is there may be intelligent life forms—mammals like us—out in the cosmos. This has caused our highest decision makers on Orthus to be serious in collecting further knowledge. All rules on this project have been arrested until we are told otherwise."

There was silence, for these technical workers were intelligent enough to know that while they may ask questions in the laboratory, they had little choice but to either work or leave the project. She said, "Those of you with strong ethical views on whether this project may cause difficulty, please leave our gathering immediately. You will have to attend a quarantine confinement by resource management." Since no one dissented, this team would do what it was trained to do.

Ana added, "Our primary task is to meticulously review our lab procedures, take sample cells of test mammals, and run through the procedures until there is no risk of losing the precious cells, if there are any. I ask that we streamline all procedural steps, and we must have complete safety from contamination. I suggest that you begin sterilization of all work hoods and ultramicroscopic pore filters and ultraviolet sterilizing lights, right down to a complete in vitro simulated environment in which we shall work away from the test samples.

"Robots involved must be reprogrammed so they respond to a step-by-step procedure. Only after careful examination of their programs will we take the next steps. There is no need for speed in this analysis of the capsule's contents. After every team is coordinated, we will be ready to undertake this project. All resources required will be available. Do not hesitate to use the best of every item needed in our armoury. There will be no second chance if one step is destroyed. Thanks for your input."

Options

The team headed by Chuck, Ra, and Sam reported that it had completed its assignment and was ready to recommend a method that would cause least damage to the contents. Chuck, who assumed the role of spokesman for this team, spoke up. "We considered three options for opening the capsule. One was using a ruby laser that would slice through one end. The second was use of a physically hardened carbon saw to slowly cut through the titanium body and avoid damage to the enclosed biological material. The third was to use a disassociation molecular charge that would allow entry through a needle hole at the spot where the integrity of the capsule would allow it."

He continued, "Using an ultra-microscope through which we could extract the internal materials, a preliminary scan would show us the type of cells with which we were dealing. However, after preliminary testing in the laboratory, the committee has decided to recommend that we use the ruby laser. The one condition is there has to be a cooling mechanism to control any heat generated on the outside of the capsule."

Ra noted, "While the ruby laser would cut through any material, and we have the spectrographic readings that reveal the capsule is made of titanium, we know that there would be a high probability of success." He felt that any microbial "traps" would have to be in the form of the hard sporulation phase of a microbe. He explained, "Any microbe in a vegetative phase would be destroyed after passing through toxic radiation that may have penetrated the capsule."

Sam, on the other hand, suggested a hypothesis of the different gauntlets that the capsule could have experienced on its journey. All worked in favour of the capsule's resilience or luck in not having met catastrophes that would have destroyed it.

Ra very thoughtfully said, "Do you think that its safety and its arrival was more focused?"

"What I mean to say is, Was it deliberately sent towards this region of the cosmos?" Sam replied. "If that were so, then it would have been directed away from major galaxies and large nuclear-fission energy from recycled suns."

Chuck intervened, saying, "Let us not think on that possibility, as evidence is lacking. Meanwhile, while that is hypothetical, a decision was made that we will open the capsule, whereupon our biological scientists will take over. We have checked all the equipment and run it for quality assurance, and it has passed successfully. Let us give our report and rejoin the subcommittee."

Subcommittee Action Meeting

Ana began, "Your reports indicate that our instruments, equipment, and safety protocols can cope with anything that the little capsule could reveal to us. We will use the suggested method of opening it with a ruby laser. Let us gather in the scientist's technologist's arena and watch as the protocol is executed. The Orthus senate has approved all our protocols; we have the approvals of the best minds, so let us begin. Our scientist leaders will monitor our systems and procedures."

Behind huge transparent titanium panels, the subcommittee members saw the little capsule lying on a black sheet. It seemed so very small and isolated when a red light was aimed at one end, which the scans revealed was hardened but had no inserted inclusions. In a split second, the end fell off. A robotic arm in the sealed, sterile atmosphere took fine forceps and slowly removed tiny capillary tubes, placing them onto a conveyor belt. And it disappeared into the molecular laboratory, where its contents were centrifuged in a high-intensity ultracentrifuge.

Tiny robotic arms removed the cells, which were microscopically examined, revealing what appeared to be biological material, still well preserved. The material was microscopically split into multiple samples, where each portion was placed into a variety of tissue cultures. This procedure had been used on the marrow cells recovered from ancient dinosaurs. The same protocol was being used now to recover viable life forms.

The ambient temperature of 30 to 36 degrees Celsius incubated these trays of tissue cultures. Huge water baths were set up in a separate growth chamber, ready for the dividing cells. As the molecular scientist began to send out the findings, there was no doubt that these were mammalian cells. Next, isolating the genetic code found that the nucleic acids were composed of only four bases—adenine, thymine, guanine, and cytosine—coiled into a double-helical link.

In the meantime, the engineers and computer experts looked at the microscopic chips. There was no doubt as to what the chips were; the experts just had to build a computer that could use these alien chips. Next, they had to read the chips and try to understand what they all meant. Were these intended as instructions and guidelines on how to bring a new life form back to their planet, or was there information asking for assistance or just a friendly gesture and communication? So much was still unknown and much had to be done. So the capsular files were spread out across the academic institutions for study and analysis.

Other inclusions and inscriptions revealed messages, using drawings to express what was wanted or needed. Here, the linguistic theorists began to assemble the inscriptions before the best scholars Orthus had. All opinions were again automatically extracted and sent to the huge library, which was otherwise open to all workers on Orthus but was now only open to these expert workers. The inscriptions were written in symbols, which were translated as follows.

Male, female, educated professionals. Two figures, male and female, holding hands. A date in cosmic time of a 24-hour day and 365 days, 1 terran year, 1 light year, $D = S \times T$ calculation. The author's library, computer chips implant cerebral patterns to physical bodies. In a diagram of human anatomy, the new life forms appeared. Time for alien language, voice interpretation, and telepathy. Details of the life form's physiological requirements—O_2, inorganic diet excretions.

Computer Chip Language

As the contents were retrieved from the capsule, non-biological samples were seen, which appeared as microscopic communication dots on the magnifier. These were passed to Chuck's committee.

It was Sam, the cosmologist, who first brought up the idea that there had to be some communication between the creators of this capsule and its intended recipients. She gave her views. "This should be of primary concern. Since an intelligent life form created this capsule, it must have some communication device or trigger within. We must look for a form of communication to explain the capsule. Everything we withdraw from the capsule may give us a clue. It will not be in a language that we understand. I suggest we search for *symbolism*.

"Maybe, with permission from our chairman, we could expose the symbols to the population of Orthus, not just the scientific community—just an idea. We would compile all suggestions in our analytics' artificial intelligence but with joint life forms of Orthusians' input. Are there any other suggestions?"

Chuck reflectively responded, "I agree with all you have said, Sam. I have nothing of any value to add. Have you any thoughts on Sam's suggestions, Ra?"

"Actually, no!" he replied to the direct question. "However, hypothetically, suppose this is not an isolated life form on a mission, but rather, for argument's sake, a robot-enslaved carbon-based life form. Could this communication be an entrapment device?"

Chuck smiled. "Really, Ra! Do you truly believe in such a scenario?"

Ra was caught in an embarrassing silence. "Truthfully, not really, but are we not to look at all possibilities, even those of a questionable, paranoid nature?"

After listening quietly, Sam replied, "I would have thought, Ra, that if this is a mammalian life form, it should carry a microbiome on some part of its anatomy. In our experience, the presence of microbiomes on all life forms, both zoological and botanical, does require the assistance of microscopic life forms to produce vital accessory growth factors that the mammalian body cannot extract. My question: Is this not a truism? Surely that would lend a greater risk to our society than a robot invasion."

"Are you questioning me about my specialty discipline, Sam?" Ra asked. "You state the obvious. Why aren't we all thinking outside our concept of 'normal' instead of going after each other's profession?" he quietly concluded.

Sam answered, "Ra, do not take my comments personally. I agree that we should think broader, and as the resident cosmologist, maybe I am failing in my discipline, and for that, I apologize."

Chuck broke in and quickly brought order to the bantering he saw taking place. "Listen, we are a small group given a terrific mandate in one of the most important tasks on Orthus. Let us not spoil this wonderful opportunity with old professional pride. It is against our Orthusian code of behaviour and professional upbringing." Silence followed.

In the meantime, Maga and Ana, in charge of the interior scans, had got together to examine the final scans before circulating them in the scientific community. Ana's team had aseptically taken out the biological material. However, Maga and Ana had little doubt in both their minds that the microscopic, highly engineered electronic dots sent to Chuck's team were the communication piece needed to guide the rest of the working subcommittee. They jointly sent a communique to members of the subcommittee, demanding that the computer engineers begin constructing the equipment necessary to read the silicon-sand chips isolated from the capsule.

Chuck, after berating his own committee for bantering, did the same, asking the two workers to keep such advice to themselves and not interfere with his small committee's mandate. Just then, a powerful telepathic voice, Saunders's internal voice, interrupted their minds:

"Members, restrict your petty differences and pride immediately. Do not let me observe such a display of beggarly professional pride again. Never forget that robots are recording every word, sentence, suggestion, even thoughts and statements made on this project for the senior senate committee to review. Please continue immediately as a full working committee."

A profound silence followed as members called to each other using telepathy to come together for the final plans.

11

CHAPTER

ROLE OF A PRIMITIVE COMPUTER

Chuck brought his team together for a progress update. "Ra, how did you manage to dig up that old screen?"

Ra, with a rare smile, said, "Well, Chuck, this is called a CRT—at least this is what the folks down at the dump and retro-recovery unit recalled from historical files. They were not happy to give it to me, as they did not have the old-fashioned printing ability to produce a copy of the internal circuits for themselves. However, these were still viable, and they showed me how to fire it up with old-fashioned electricity. They allowed me to turn it on, but to use a transformer on the electric current."

Ra's excitement as he carefully handled the antique piece was palpable. He had his team's full attention. "Since we do not have that old utility available, they gave me a black box called a *battery* that works as the energy source. It works, for they had some old disposable USB storage tubes with history files that were recorded for the library. The librarian once insisted they never were to destroy these USB devices that millions of workers generations ago used to record their work details. Later on, the librarian composed many documents into print—now, of course, into air documents stored in an electronic guarded space at the library."

Chuck laughed out loudly and said, "You had quite an adventure, but thanks. First, let me tell you and Sam what I did at the library. After being granted permission, I went over all the stored documents on the history of old computing functions. It seems that we also shrunk down major catalogues of our history and achievements into microdots, where literally billions of documents on Orthus's history and its achievements are stored."

Sam interrupted, "You mean that you got through to the librarian's deepest history-storage airspace unit?"

"Yes." Chuck, who continued, laughed out. "The best part was when I told her that we had retrieved what we believe is a microdot that may contain information from the capsule. She was ecstatic."

Ra asked, "Did you get to meet Dia, the mysterious librarian?"

Chuck, full of pride at his achievement, burst out with enthusiasm. "Not only did I meet her, but she remained close when I entered the depths of her old storage units. She showed me millions of stored documents and their storage units, as well as the devices used to recover the details, since many are ancient and quite fragile. They could not be transferred to newer equipment for fear of losing the documents' integrity. Using my portable recorder, I showed her the microscopic microdot that we have in our laboratory."

He paused for a moment then continued, "Dia was shocked and quietly raised her hand to stop me from speaking. I obeyed, for she looked stunned and her eyes widened. Slowly, she walked away from me, beckoning me to follow her."

"An hour or more later, she stopped after many electronic stairs downwards, speaking not even a telepathic warning came from her. We arrived at a cool dungeon of a place with old-fashioned doors and locks as seen in the storybooks of my childhood. After opening the strange doors, Dia spoke for the first time.

'Engineer Chuck, I have a device here that could read your microdot. I believe that it still functions, for my older robo-staff looks after these very old sections and equipment. I can get them to set it up and have it running if you would bring the microdot processor here. We will place it directly into the old equipment that would read your old files. When can you bring the microdot to me?'"

Chuck laughed and paused. "I now see the cunning of that librarian—"

Sam interrupted, "Why do you not let us all go there and see her translate the hidden codes?" Chuck said nothing for a long time as Sam quietly looked on, wondering what his problem was. Her subcommittee leader no longer looked directly at her but stared down at his feet.

It was Ra who quietly spoke next. "It is our project, and we are bound by a policy of maintaining that part of the capsule. Should it ever leave our trust or be destroyed outside our laboratory, we will be held responsible. Dia will immediately hide behind not having known the consequences. In fact, how do we know that she would translate the details of the microdot, since we do not have her skills? It is possible that she will tell us it did not work and she will store its information under her security codes, where no one would ever be able to access or find it."

There was silence as he continued. "She could store it as an artefact found by our cosmic scavengers and have it kept in her deepest archives. None in the senate would go after her, for she is invulnerable. Chuck would have the duty of explaining why he acted so poorly. I am not saying that the magnificent Dia would be that devious, but how could we ever know? None of us knows how to use this machine, so we could not tell whether it was working or not, but Dia would know."

Just as Ra finished giving his opinion, Chuck seemed to wake up and spoke deliberately. "Sam, this would be easy if we did what you suggest. We must curb our enthusiasm. And thank you, Ra, for your explanation to Sam, but I have been mentally wrestling with how to communicate with the powerful librarian, Dia."

Sam realized her impetuous suggestion could cause them all great angst under the planet's leaders. Her mind wandered into the great, deep blackness of space, where she mentally hid when all seemed intolerable. But suddenly, she had a thought. "You know, Chuck, you could tell her truthfully that planetary policy forbids you from removing the microdot from the safe sanctuary of our laboratory but you are willing to send two members of your subcommittee to learn how to use the old equipment and to run test samples as part of the training. Of course, she would have to allow the machine to be moved from the library to our laboratory, but only she would train us. What do you think?"

Chuck seems to come awake. "Sam, I had thought of that scenario on my way back here, but she would not do that in a million star years. Never will she allow any pieces of equipment to leave her library, eespecially those held in the ancient section where I was led. She protects those cold, frightening caverns with great authority—and security software that would destroy an intruder."

Ra interrupted, "Look, this is circuitous. Maybe I should revisit the garbage collection personnel and seek an antique computer such as Dia has in her antique storage. If you could ascertain what her microdot reader is like, we can search for it."

Just then, Dia mentally transmitted to the subcommittee that she would be interested in meeting with Chuck and his subcommittee. "If your committee agrees, Chuck, how about early tomorrow morning? Let me know what you decide. I shall enter my meditation state for the evening. You can use that to connect with me," she quietly stated.

No one spoke as Chuck and Ra began to look over the old central processing unit (CPU) and cathode-ray tube (CRT) from a curiosity perspective. Chuck then spoke in a happier tone. "You know, playing around with this old technology could be quite absorbing. What do you think?"

Sam quietly demurred. "I guess we will meet Dia tomorrow morning. No one would dare refuse the great librarian who volunteered to meet us in our laboratory."

Chuck held a printed circuit board in his hands while Ra keenly looked on and said, "Her request was rhetorical. Now, I have to welcome her or be struck down in a mental fit. Yes, we shall be here but keep the microdot behind the thick, unbreakable glass with the ultra-sterilization and filter unit on full blast. All of us will be wearing filter masks and white self-sterilizing laboratory coats. Sam, would you order one to fit our librarian visitor? Thanks."

Sam and Ra, the chosen workers in different fields of expertise, found common ground to work together on their antique CPU. They were having fun learning about and discovering all the different microchips of yesteryear. Once they had taken the instrument apart, they reassembled it. They knew they could do the same for the microdot CPU.

Sam quietly stated, "Well, that was interesting. Let us bring up that era from our knowledge tutor and ask to see how those early machines worked and how we can rebuild one for our project."

Ra broke in, "Let us have the tutor functioning when Dia arrives in the morning so she can see how determined we are to go it without any assistance."

With their enthusiasm for the plan to save time with the library's ancient microdot reader, the task force's chairman called in through the photo-communication screen. They and Chuck stopped work and turned to see the face of Chairman Kha. "Chuck, I have heard from our robots all that your team has accomplished to date. By the way, I also heard of your latest plans. Sorry about that. I was about to make contact when the robot keyed your laboratory on audio before the photo."

The chairman continued. "I signalled that it should pause until I heard every bit of your plan. All I can say is good luck with Dia. Now, the good news on the capsule is we have isolated a piece of what looks like an incisor root, based on our diagnostic magnification. The molecular biology laboratory has had great success in isolating the aged tissue's DNA. Indeed, it is designing a biological soma that would hold the beginnings of a mammalian form. The biological baths used for the return of the dinosaurs have been modified. The biologists will now search further for other remnants of nucleic acids. Just an update."

Chuck called his two partners together. "It will be possible for the molecular workers to postulate what the body shape would look like from their molecular patterns. We may be able to get a more precise idea from the inscriptions given to us. We need to move ahead quicker than we have been doing."

Sam responded, "Then what is the plan?"

Chuck replied, "I believe that we should work through the night and bring in the technical assistance immediately."

Ra volunteered, "I will collect a team immediately and bring them back. I will tell them to work until the task is completed."

Chuck responded, "Let us move ahead, Sam I will like you to stay and work with me on these parts. Get the 3D printer, and load it with silica so we can duplicate these chips. I will load the pattern structure using the X-ray differentiator."

Meanwhile, across the planet, where the huge library was situated, Dia spoke to her companion robot after ensuring that they would be safe from listening or spying. "You know, Robot, my hearing investigators have slipped information to me that my piece of instrumentation is badly needed to open and interpret the symbols from a microdot silica chip taken from the alien capsule." She spoke quietly to the warm robot designed specifically for her delight and companionship. It looked like her double, but its programming was one of logic and sensitivity.

Robot murmured softly before saying in a soft, husky voice, "Does that bother you, my dear Dia?"

Dia quickly replied, "What do you think? Of course it does. I do not want to be left out because of my reputation as being difficult to work with, which gossiping professionals have given me."

Robot quickly responded, "No need to take it out on me, your dear companion. Anyway, you are obviously distressed, so why not take advantage of this opportunity and carry the microdot instrument with you to their lab and surprise them? Tell them you will be an ex officio member of their subcommittee. Offer to assist them to record the symbols. But of more importance, bring the power of the library resources in assisting in their interpretation for the population of Orthus. What do you think of such a plan, my dear Dia?"

Dia paused and stilled her overworked mind. There was silence—not a sound—and the companion that usually interrupted also remained quiet but with a wicked smile on its countenance. Dia then spoke unhurriedly. "What a wonderful companion you are, Robot. Let us begin right away. Call the technologists and repair staff, and have them meet me at the engineer's laboratory." Robot rose from the chair and disappeared to immediately fulfil Dia's wishes.

Chuck was surprised at an interruption that a visitor was waiting to meet him with a team. He asked his prompter who the visitor was, but before it could respond, Dia and her team materialized in front of him and Sam. Chuck came forward. "This is most unusual, even for you, Dia. Why are you here? This lab is out of bounds to everyone but research staff that Chairman Kha approved."

Dia took over at once; most folks avoided her because of her authoritative attitude. "Chuck, you came to me to look at the microdot antique. I made the offer to teach you and your subcommittee staff how to use the instrument. I now withdraw my offer, and instead, I would like to be part of your working applied team. I can save you a great deal of time. I have brought the instrument and the service staff so we can begin testing the sample in your lab right away, under your direction. I promise to bring the full resources of the planet's library to begin the interpretative process, if you would let me."

She paused, and then, with her quick mind, she told him, "Call back Ra from the disposal group, where he is hunting through a lot of junk. That is wasting valuable time."

This left Chuck completely baffled, and his instinct took over. "Great to have your assistance, Dia, but I am in charge of this piece of the project. Would you agree to work under my direction and that of my committee members?"

At this interlude in their discussion, Robot took over to reply for Dia. "But of course, dear engineer Chuck, we just wish to be part of the team to quickly bring this aspect to reality. After all, the senate committee told you to use the planetary resources to get this task done. Our library is the largest consolidated resource on the planet and probably in the universe. We may one day have to expand our services to other life forms when they are discovered in the cosmos."

Chuck asked directly, "Does your companion robot speak for you in every detail, Dia?"

"Of course. Robot is the only partner who understands me and remains loyal to my mission. However, our library belongs to the universe, not just planet Orthus," Dia replied.

Ra was recalled, and on the way, he was made aware of the unexpected offer and the arrival of the library's technical staff. He paused at a communication booth and whispered a message. Lights flickered as all the recording and robotic communication devices became alert with the message, sharing symbolic drawings he had found.

> Male and female physical shapes with a head, hands, legs, genitals, eyes, and a mouth; eating and speaking actions; ancient language; Latin and English arias; popular songs; love; docile eyes; hugging adults; a baby from a womb; a DNA double helix; different colours; mating, writing, and laughing; growing old and dying.

Chuck's team was completely dumbfounded by the drawings, which were sent across the whole planet and arrived at the senior senate, hidden away in the caves on Orthus.

12

CHAPTER

AN ALIEN APPEARS

In Ana's laboratory, a great deal of redesigning had taken place for the alien's physical appearance. The scientists knew they were working with an intelligent life form. They also assumed that the capsule had more directions for dealing with its interpretation. Ana was convinced that the alien was not a barbaric race but a genuine civilized life form in search of other life forms.

Ana was aware that the leaders of Orthus had decided several decades ago to stop looking for other life forms with whom they wished to communicate. The old members of the senior senate had reviewed the huge investment in their search and decided that continuing it at that time had no benefit. They had polled the population's leaders, and it was decided to call off all future searches for other viable mammalian beings in their universe.

As a student of the molecular bioscience, Ana was involved in recovering the prehistoric mammals that at one time roamed their mighty planet, long before their own bipedal species evolved. Because of Orthus's massive size and Orthusians' self-restricted growth, large land spaces were left as grand parks to house these projects; Orthusian parks were set aside so the giants of the past could live safely away from civilization's development.

After many years, she saw the trials that took place after the in vitro growth of cells from ancient frozen tissues taken from ice-trapped prehistoric animals. This was followed by the isolation of the different species' DNA. Once isolated and living, DNA was inserted in the process, and many species were brought back to life and released into their old surroundings. This massive undertaking had a major fault; it impaired the species' natural reproduction. It had been common knowledge among geneticists that such genetic rebirths from tissue culture had this side effect. Even if a successful birth took place, the offspring did not survive the first year.

That project continued under a full team of scientists that included molecular biologists, ecosystem development analysts, ethics and other academics. Ana did not wish to be part of that project, so she kept to the pure development of her science. Her expertise was now required for this challenging project that had come from outer space, the great cosmos.

There was value in waiting for the right time to indulge one's great passion in Orthusian society. However, lack of support by the head scientists had drained this discipline of its resources. She was unable to fight through the bureaucracy even when she made significant scientific progress.

She quietly said to herself, *If we Orthusians, as a species, have come from such a wonderful evolution to build a well-developed society, then what should be our purpose?*

If the purpose was to only accumulate information and knowledge, solve complicated scientific and social problems, and then store these accomplishments as knowledge, then one had to ask, *To what end? If it is for just the purity of knowledge, then are we not just as sterile as our new dinosaurs?*

Just as Ana was about to become upset, Maga walked into the room, looked at her sharply, and said, "You should turn off the thought and mental transmitters when you get into these moods. I heard your mental questioning, and it is safe to conclude your questions may have been forwarded to the old senate. Be careful of what you are thinking; you may inadvertently put up barriers, my dear colleague, when you begin to soliloquize."

Shocked, Ana looked up and quickly replied, "You know, Maga, I really do not care who listens to my thoughts. I would not be surprised if you had similar thoughts yourself. Maybe our leaders have gone to sleep." She paused.

After walking around the lab and looking at tissue-culture vats secured behind thick, sterile, translucent quarantine barriers, she picked up her train of thought. "The leaders have not reopened our planetary search for other life forms in the great cosmos. As a result, I believe they have become afraid of what they might find. This, in turn, is also making us younger scientists afraid of the facts that lie out there. Truthfully, I believe that an immortal, powerful being must oversee the workings of the cosmos. The purity of the great universe could not be left to its created beings, such as those of us who have evolved. I understand that this type of thinking is sacrilege in our society, but really, I do not care."

Maga saw her colleague's meltdown and replied, "The trouble, Ana, is that you care too much. Our leaders must think freshly on where our civilization has to focus our population's energy for the future, or else we will be unprepared when the future arrives. Maybe, just maybe this alien will come to life through the workings of your team. Only then shall we be sure that an immortal being indeed sent us this stimulus to think, for that is exactly what is needed." Silence followed as the two scientists looked at each other.

Looking at her colleague, Ana responded, "I never thought of it that way. You have provided me with all the stimulus I need to recreate this alien life form and become its friend. Its future survival will demand a team to look after its welfare. We have the knowledge. Now, we must learn to communicate with an alien life form. What a wonderful prospect to speak to an intelligent being and search its mind for wisdom. Just maybe, it may have a different outlook from its own beginnings and it would be nice to have it regurgitate its history and past evolution to our population."

With bright enthusiasm, Ana added, "I will be its friend and colleague. I will fight for its survival with my team of experts, and we will use this planet's resources to keep it in existence for my lifetime. Hopefully, I will convince another to take over when I can no longer do it. Tonight, I shall begin looking at its DNA and the physiological parameters of this alien life form."

Maga expressed her opinion, "When Chuck and his team uncover the probable structure of the soma, then as with the dinosaurs, we will be able to key in what the internal organs may do within and thereby allow the being to survive. We would also like to know about the displacement of organs within the body."

Ana smiled. "Thanks, Maga. You will join my team in this daring mission?"

"With your guidance; no way will I go it alone. Of course, I will join your team," Maga replied. "You know, Ana, from the historical scans that I have, my computer could maybe postulate the most efficient location of the internal organs' displacement. The missing parameters would be how much gravity and what gaseous conditions this alien being will require," she concluded with a look of puzzlement.

The two scientists separated, then hurried away at a pace not seen on the planet for many years. They had awakened new determination and excitement, which would spread across the planet as protocols circulated uncensored information.

Maga brought her team up to date on all that she had discussed with Ana. She then asked if the team members would voluntarily join her on the molecular team. She painted a future where all the sciences would eventually combine to awaken a life form. The excitement would come from knowing whether it was a civilized being from a location deep in the cosmos.

It did not take long for logic to take over and sensible deductions to be made. As the team worked out the details, the members became excited at the prospect of seeing a life form from the cosmos and from another planet.

Chuck and his team, composed of a microbiologist and the cosmologist, now accepted Dia and her team as team members. Dia brought out her ancient microdot interpreter, and with subdued excitement, she ran the controls, and the machine, under her careful, delicate touch, responded positively. Dia stopped and then called all to attention as she postulated. "Chuck, there is the possibility that the machine may spit out its interpretation using our symbols, which would appear as gibberish. There is no knowledge prognosticated that would have a complete design for an alien of unknown physiology and anatomy."

Profound silence followed in the lab space as reality set in for the small group. Sam, the cosmologist, broke the silence. "That is true, as none of our planet's past exploits have ever found anything that could be considered truly alien. Using our limited knowledge based on our own makeup, we know little as far as language or a worldwide standard of language, physiology, anatomy, and temperament that might exist."

Heads nodded as Chuck intervened. "It is good to have spelt out Sam, but that does not help us with this dilemma.

"Wait a minute!" exclaimed Ra. "Why not? Yes, of course." He seemed to speak to himself. He approached the electronic diagram board; with the magnetic chalk, he drew the three physical shapes of bacteria. He looked at his focused team. "You see, I have a huge collection of microbes in my stock cultures, which were microfilmed through scanning microscopes. They all have a few things in common."

He looked at the diagram and then said, "Our early explorers' journals from their journey into outer space describe what they saw amid the darkness and distant light flashes, which they referred to as *galaxies*. They collected samples of soil matter and space dust and brought them back. The early microbiologists found microbes, which they isolated. The explorers drew maps of where they obtained these isolates in different parts of the universe. Granted, their journey was limited, though it provided a sampling of the makeup of the cosmos."

Ra closed his eyes then as if to recall something. "Samples of microbes were collected from dead, frozen planets and from 'living planets' with lots of liquid methane that had viable bacteria. Others were isolated from extremely hot planets with active volcanic eruptions still violent. There were large metallic planets that were difficult to get to because of the intense gravity that they exuded. Microbial isolates were also recovered from planets that had a range of gaseous mixtures in different atmospheres and gravitational pressures."

Dia interrupted, "Ra, collect all the data on your microbial isolates. Have the computer align the physical conditions with those from which the microbes were isolated. Extrapolate similarities under each parameter, such as those isolates from extreme environmental conditions, and place such a group into one category. Summarize the conditions so we can inform the molecular group of how we found microbial life forms under a range of cosmic conditions. The group could then take it from there and test a few of the alien cells until it finds optimal conditions for cell proliferation."

She stopped as Chuck continued in the same vein. "Then, the molecular group is to challenge the alien tissue under different conditions just to test the tissue's tolerance and ability to survive under suboptimal conditions as well as maximally grow under lab-defined conditions."

Hardly had he finished when their minds were called into focus as Elder Chairman Saunders telepathically messaged, "Well done, subcommittee, under astrophysics leader Chuck and team. Very clever of you all to include her highness Dia on the team. Dia, can you have your computers collect the molecular biologists' feedback? Indeed, you have the greatest computers on Orthus; it is about time they were brought online to work on this project."

Saunders went silent, then slowly added, "Let all the information to date, including that of the initial meeting, feed into their memory banks. Let them search the library books, many of which have been accumulated for the better part of a billion years—key in the search of the cosmos. Also, look at our own evolution as that of a successful model, abstract, comparative carbon-based life forms. Direct the computers to not only extrapolate but go into postulations and hypotheses for all to share. Begin now, and the workers on this project are not to delay or have resting phases."

He stopped then continued, "You should all know that molecular genetic miracle now has a tenor of urgency. This work is being shared with every Orthusian, and the public pressure has given completion a profound political importance that threatens to redefine our future."

Ana looked into the huge tissue-culture baths that were designed for a life form similar in size to an average Orthusian. She worked on stats of three metres in height and about one metre across the shoulders with no extended upper appendages. She knew that within two solar months a whole being could be made.

A cellular frame made out of botanical tissue was designed as an Orthusian body. However, as the alien's cells grew, the growth actually redefined the conditions, causing the computers to adapt to unknown requirements of temperature, pH, gas, and atmospheric pressure measured on a gravity scale.

As the conditions evolved, almost-visibly changes propelled maximal growth of the cells. Ana was speechless as her staff stood around in silence. They watched as the computers took over. But for some unknown reason, the alien cells with their genetic codes twisted into a double helix of defined nucleic acids. It appeared that instructions were fed back to the tissue-culture parameters and automatically adjusted. All her staff could do was follow through, ensuring that they fed what was needed in unfettered amounts into the laboratory's controlled conditions.

13

CHAPTER

AN ALIEN'S PHYSICAL FORM

The team observed the alien's head, the tissue organs inside the figure, the circulatory pumping of fluid, the circulation of air, and the alien's foot mobility. The figure had upper appendages for holding, handling, and pressing.

Chuck spoke out. "Well, it is not too far removed from our structure. We do not know what the smaller appendages are at the ends of the upper and lower large appendages."

The team again stared in silence, then gasped in awe. Dia's mind became feverish as thoughts raced through her head. "My goodness, there are other life forms similar to us in the cosmos. They are trying to communicate with us. What arrogance and sophistication and excitement for they are communicating with other life forms in the universe at a base level of tissue cultures."

Dia gasped, a most unusual reflex for this tower of strength. "We are an accident on Orthus. We are here more by luck than by design, and we have received their device that supports our primitive evolution. We are not the clever ones; there are more advanced civilizations out there. This does not portend well for our leaders. They are faced with the dilemma of having a communication and probably a biological life form with an intelligence that surpasses our own."

Suddenly, a strange response for this race of a dourer temperament began to take place. Wild laughter broke out, which frightened everyone. Dia jumped up and screamed and did a strange dance of delight. "They could not travel here, so they sent their bio-form as tissue cells in the hope that an advanced civilization would recreate their life form away from their own solar system. How remarkably clever! We must bring that life form back as a living intelligent creature and protect its existence. This is when our knowledge will begin to expand and our lives will change for the better."

Sam looked on with great shock on her face. "Team members, we are very fortunate to have probably seen the physical shape of an alien on the planet under our control. However, several things come to mind should we wake this developed physical being, for we must assume that was the intention when the capsule was launched. If we do, what form of communication or skill will it have? Of more importance, will we be able to understand its needs?"

She continued, "How will we recognize its behaviour as beastly or kind or non-savage? What diseases does it carry within its developed physical form? Does it have a message for us or for any others that might be out there in the cosmos? Will that message be universal or intended for a specific group of life forms other than us? So many questions and no answers. Where are our noble senators, the aged who are supposed to provide direction to our population possibly allaying all fears or apprehensions to a stage of comfort?"

It was Ra's turn, and he spoke loudly. "All that has been said and thought about is quite true. We are the ones that found the capsule, so what does that indicate? Are we the intended society this life form sought? If microbes exist throughout the cosmos under varying conditions, from extreme to moderate, why would this life form not be similar and able to exist on our planet? I believe that we must bring this life form back to a living biological state as soon as possible."

Suddenly, their minds were focused by a powerful telepathic interruption. "Subcommittee members, you are all on the correct path. However, rather than focusing on circumspection, why not focus on the pseudo-tangibles, such as hypothetical conditions for existence on planet Orthus? Its physiology now demands that there be a draft of its anatomy. What does it need for nourishment?"

After some silence, an inspired continuation took place. "Get our food scientists here, and have them look into what is needed to keep the alien body healthy. We have the moral responsibility to see this being brought to life, and it is our planetary mandate to keep it safe and healthy."

Dia was shocked as she called out, "This alien life form is a living library of information that could provide much about part of the cosmos of which we have no knowledge. This is an exciting time for all Orthusians. Let the schools of our youths be exposed to the diagram of the life form, and let them try to explain its living requirements. They may use our physiology and anatomy as a guideline to begin. Later on, they can develop any extra requirements deemed necessary for its continued healthy existence.

"To our youth, there is no such thing as bad information or useless suggestions and hypotheses. We will collect, analyse, and store everything for the future, when it may come in handy in solving other problems that may arise. Let the full team work together, for that is a directive from the senior senate. This is a planetary operation, and all resources must be used to achieve our goal of inviting this alien ambassador from across the cosmos to come and live with us.

"Astrophysics leader Chuck and the biologist group, there is a piece of technology missing. It has been taken out of the capsule. It looks like the imprint of neural patterns. Look into why this was included and its possible use. We suggest that you will only need one copy, which will be sent to you, as it is encoded in fragile material."

Information began to flow from all sections across Orthus. Biology instructors to the planetary population focused on the youth still at academies. One instructor told her students, "One can only make assumptions based on our own physiology. We are born of an ovum from a female fertilized by a male sperm cell. Even though there maybe differences between different races on our planet, we are the same species. The principle is the same for mammals, of which the basic truths are we will all grow old eventually, our external body will change and we will die.

"While we are alive, our body does incredible work to keep our brain, our nervous system, and our physical state healthy and productive. For example, we have a fluid that circulates around our insides, which assists in the intake and excretion of products from our diet and in our respiration. This is pumped by the great muscle in our chest cavity, thus allowing nutrients from our diet to be deposited at sites that require rebuilding of our muscles, nerves, and skeletal framework."

After checking her lecture facts on a prompter, the instructor said, "Some facts on the history of our race: Our biological height has been stable at around three to four metres tall. Our weight has been kept at around eighty kilograms, plus or minus ten kilograms, except when the females are bearing a foetus."

The youths' class uncovered a few truths of their own race as Orthusians, including the following.

- Because of Orthusians' height and weight, their internal circulatory muscle pumps eight thousand litres of fluid around their body every day of their lives. That is more than a few hundred times per day. That muscle contracts more than one hundred thousand times daily.
- Two huge air bags in Orthusians' chest, which contract without their thinking, control respiration. They inhale oxygen and

produce carbon dioxide that they expel over twenty thousand times daily.

- Orthusians' body structures are made up of numerous types of cells. Like all living parts, if their DNA strands did not keep under strict control, many deviations in cell structure would occur, causing abnormal growths that could spread throughout the body, causing premature death.
- Orthusians' digestive tract stays under keen metabolic neural control lest the digestive acids begin to digest their insides.
- Orthusians' seeing organs in their head bathe their eyes at least thirty times daily to keep any contaminants from entering and causing damage or infection.
- Orthusians' body covering is an organ, and it is replaced daily, for it is made up of millions of cells that die and fall off. This ensures that Orthusians remain healthy and free of bodily eruptions.
- Orthusians' brain and verbal communication work together to pass ideas and thoughts to a few select individuals and also to the planet's hierarchy.
- Orthusians' internal organs are responsible for the assimilation of nutrients and the removal of toxic by-products of digestion. The internal organs are also responsible for the excretion of wastes after digestion, thereby maintaining Orthusians' health.
- Orthusians' organs are replaced at the cellular level without Orthusians' being conscious of this ongoing rebuilding and replacement.

In conclusion, the biology instructor said, "These facts should be the same for every existing life form from the simplest unicellular microbe to the most complex adult of all mammalian species.

However, these facts only relate to carbon-based life forms, for those are the only life forms we know. For further information on Orthusian physiology and anatomical development, seek information from the great library."

14

CHAPTER

MORE FACTS ABOUT ORTHUSIAN BODIES

Dia then spoke to her team members. "While what the biology instructor said about us is quite true, we must remember that while the principles may be similar, this is an alien being. Its needs will be different; for instance, we do not know whether its own environment has the same mixture of air that our does, even while it may have gases similar to H_2, O_2, N_2, and CO_2, and trace amounts of neon, argon, et cetera. We should all remember that there is a very narrow bridge between being alive and living optimally."

Dia continued in a more contemplative mood in discussion with her teammates. "The questions that we must ask are simple enough, such as, at what concentration are these gases present on the alien's planet? Next, what role do the botanical species play on its planet? On Orthus, the botanical life forms are inextricably tied to the zoological species. Do they have massive oceans of methane or of salt water? Furthermore, what botanical species live in these oceans? Are these primates dependent on these species? If not, how are they interrelated? Finally, what gravity pressure is exerted on its alien planet? I am sure that you scientists have many more questions.

"Cautiously, I ask that we all remember this alien is a most precious ambassador, not unlike the president of this planet. We must show respect for another living being from a distant galaxy or solar system. Furthermore, we must attend to all its survival needs without the need for any administrative approval process."

Chuck said to Dia, "You have stated the obvious to all of us, and we know our responsibility on this project. But something more appears to be bothering you, Dia, something almost foreboding. What is it?" The team members gathered around and enclosed the librarian, who had such power that only the president of Orthus could ask her for a favour.

Dia kept the library of knowledge in both animate and inanimate forms so that the whole population of the planet could access any and all information without censure. The planet's evolution from tribal communities to the complex unified population was aware of this free resource. Millions of documents traced how past leaders designed policies that had brought the harmony that Orthusians experienced today. From simple social aspects of justice to complicated policies passed by law, the planet's lawmakers and ethics committees could refer to Dia's library for clarity. She had done all this by building an impregnable, detailed collection of works dating back to Orthusians' prehistory.

She was admired, for she could find any document or device just as quickly as the robots could. Of more importance, she would freely add a summary or her opinion on the positive and negative aspects of any document she was asked to find. Scientists, medical experts, and lawyers all came to her for supportive documentation and actively sought her opinion.

There was silence even when the robotic and automatic devices quietly documented every word spoken, every thought involved with this project. Finally, Dia replied, "You see, Chuck, everyone is keen to see the alien living and running around as the animals do in our large parks where we keep show animals and plants for our young and aged to study and enjoy. This is not the same, and I distrust our leaders to see that this life form is not for show."

Looking at her team she expounded, "This is an intelligent alien that has reached out from a distant planet that must have been created as ours was. Whether or not it came here intentionally does not matter. It is our responsibility to protect it, give it our respect, and be good hosts."

She thoughtfully continued, "We are the generation of Orthusians that will meet an intelligent alien life form from the great cosmos for the first time. Yes, our technology and our skills can bring it back, and we will work out the biological details on how to keep it safe. But this being will not know our language, and it may not be able to use telepathy to communicate with us. It is our responsibility to take the initiative to learn to communicate with this life form."

"However, in doing so, we shall have to learn a new language. In turn, we will gain insight into a new culture, a new evolutionary history that will most likely be unlike anything we have ever known or could postulate. As a librarian who stores knowledge for our population and for any population that would come to us, can you imagine the great importance that is being foisted on us—on me?"

Dia went quiet, which was unusual for this powerful individual, as she had kept that powerful façade for many years. Ra clearly spoke up. "Dia, what shall we do? We must work with the molecular specialists to bring the alien back as a living entity. That is a fact, and really, we have no choice. In doing so, we must have guidelines from our ethics consultant, but again, our ethics might not be universal for all life forms. We must not treat this like one of our wild animals. Wild animals do not write in code or draw symbols for interpretation. We know that this is an intelligent life form, and we must treat it with great respect, but how ... where do we begin?"

A DECISION:

In a loud voice, Dia spoke up, and the sound of her voice brought everyone to attention. "Leaders of Orthus, we must immediately put together a dedicated body of devoted individuals who will protect this alien life form. I want to be on that committee. Be prepared, dear leaders of Orthus, for if any injustice is shown to this alien, I shall lead the charge for severe penalties, from the simplest inappropriate slights to overt rudeness to a visitor."

Shouting physically as well as through her immense telepathic mind, she raged. "These laws must be among the toughest that our constitution has. We must design new laws to protect this alien being. All those of a similar opinion, please contact me and provide your qualifications to be on such a policy committee. This will be not just be a committee of policies and language but an armed force that will use its powers to keep our visitor free from all harm. Orthusians might die if they dare offend this entity from the cosmos."

With that, she left with her staff and librarian robots.

The senate committee was a group of elder statesmen numbering twelve. As they died off, they were replaced by other elders. Their collective wisdom was deemed essential to sensibly running the planetary leadership under a president.

In response to Dia's words, Senator A said to the other senate committee members, "Am I to believe that our dynamic librarian has challenged us to behave according to rules that she feels strongly about?"

Senator C replied, "That is correct, for she feels that we will treat this reawakened alien life form similar to the way we have done with our ancient dinosaurs. It does not say much for our advice to the leadership of Orthus."

Senator D added, "Well, all citizens have a right to give their opinions, and our very powerful librarian has done so, as a citizen of Orthus with a strong opinion on this project. She does have a good opinion on the need to treat this alien as an important visitor from the universe—a representative, so to speak, not just a visitor—since we did not previously find any evidence of similar life forms to ourselves as being mammals."

Finally, senator B chimed in. "I have remained silent while opinions have been expressed. We must take Dia's comments seriously for two major reasons. Our law must have an ethical standard, currently unwritten, on how to treat such a life form. It is not a savage animal, for it brought its own message with it. This being is, in fact, guiding us on how to bring it back to a physical state. That would suggest it had a premonition that a developed civilization would find its capsule and make the transformation. While this is conjecture on my part at this stage, it is a fact that we have never been prepared for such an event. We must take it seriously, and it should be treated as an ambassador to Orthus."

Senator F's thoughts differed. He said, "I have severe reservations, and while I do not disagree with all that has been said, I would like to put forward a different hypothesis. My reasoning is, should we have to develop policies to address this life form as a civilized being similar to us, it is indeed necessary to take precautions. These will be built into the document. However, in the event that the life form becomes a threat and reacts in a deviant and unexpected manner, what happens then?"

He coughed then continued, "It is not my intent or suggestion that Orthusians treat all aliens as gentle, when, in fact, there may be aggressive aliens. Yes! I know it came in its parts assuming that we would behave as we currently are doing."

He coughed again then went on. "Suppose this is the molecular part of an alien life form that has an incurable illness that could infect our unprotected and susceptible populations. Indeed, it is possible that the remnants of this life form could carry a microbe that has the potential to destroy the whole population of our planet. Suppose this is a criminal deviant of a society that handles its chronic prisoners by sending them into outer space. There are other scenarios, but you all get the gist of my caution and paranoia."

He paused before adding, "I am perturbed by the strong opinion that Dia expressed, almost a threat to us all in the leadership. She should be cautioned and told to lower the tone of her confrontation."

Senator G said, "And who in this senate is willing to take on our librarian in a verbal and political battle in an attempt to bring her into line for her non-confrontational approach? I can assure you, senators, that I am too old and have absolutely no stomach for such a task. On the other hand, we could agree on exactly what she would like us to do. I suggest that we ask her to be in charge of a board of governors such as SHAHLA."

"There, she will receive the resources required to keep the alien as a member of the Librarian Assets. She will not allow the alien to be used as a showpiece for our population; it will be an ambassador from a foreign planet. She can select a team that will be devoted to the alien's survival and partial integration into Orthusian philosophy and society. We will exchange our history, science, and general way of life and living in exchange that will share the knowledge, history and philosophy of its own planetary civilization."

Senator B replied, "Actually, that is a quite a devious suggestion, and I rather like it. In such an organizational construct, we will make only one demand—that she keep us informed. Her subcommittee does all the work, and if anything goes wrong with the alien's health, or there are threats to its survival, we just have to set up an enquiry and let the law of Orthus take its course."

Senator A asked, "Are there any other suggestions or opinions that would remove this task from our agenda? If not, let us have a motion to set in place the last recommendation."

The old senators never had their decisions or discussions open to any other Orthusian. They were free to discuss all alternatives without dissent or censure from Orthusian society. Their opinions were never questioned, for they were the aged, full of wisdom that one could not teach and could only attain through living a long life and holding a prominent position on a planetary council.

So they gave the task to Dia, but little did they appreciate what Dia had in mind. It was a grave mistake, for soon, their wholly unchallenged position revealed its vulnerability.

15
CHAPTER

AN ALIEN IS REBORN

Within the huge tanks once used to bring back the dinosaurs using DNA obtained in eggs and bones from archaeological collections, a new experiment had to be developed and after many repeats was successful. Only now, a figure of less than two metres was developed from tissue cells, which had brought instructions within their capsule. The figure had a head and four appendages—two attached to the upper body, two at the lower end of the body. It appeared to be of a light brown colour with black hair on its top and at its lower end between the two lower appendages.

It also had five smaller appendages on each upper limb and lower limb. It had two side-by-side unopened openings on the head, two smaller openings in the middle of the head, and a small opening under these two small openings. There were two epidermal projections, one on each side of the head, with holes in them as well. It was not an unpleasant sculpture—rather, one that an artist sculptor could design—but this was a much more complicated anatomical figure than an Orthusian.

The scanning computers had given an idea of the internal organs and their displacement. An internal bone network, not unlike Orthusians', appeared to hold up the outer dermis. A red fluid circulated around in millions of tiny vessels, removing CO_2 and leaving O_2 at the musculature sites. Two large tissue organs took in the air, which had been worked out to be 20 per cent O_2, 70 per cent N_2, and 10 per cent CO_2. The face had closed seeing organs and a breathing pendulum.

It was a whole being, an alien life form living in the tank. Chuck and his team arrived with a microscopic chip made of biosilica sent through a sterile tube. He allowed it to float into the tank. Then microcomputers, using delicate surgical robots, inserted the chip into the alien's head. A microelectric current started the life movement by inserting needle like probes through the still-soft skull. This was not new, for this type of surgical procedure was routinely done on Orthusians who had obtained brain damage through either sports or adventures on dangerous geological outcroppings.

The teams anxiously watched as the naked torso, just under two metres, floated, taking in nutrients through a cord connected to its indented belly. The alien body twitched at the small stimuli. The robots watched and measured, then slowly increased the shock, observing more jerks as the torso pitched to and fro within the tank. A pause was called for upon further current increases as the scientists looked at the charts and became apprehensive that damage to the still-fragile tissue-cultured alien might occur

They gathered around the large computer screen, looking at the physiological functioning results as it affected parts of its anatomy.

The breathing-gaseous mixture appeared to be correct, but at present it was still being abstracted from the surrounding growth solution. Radiometric examination scans revealed functioning lungs, a pump that caused the fluid to flow throughout the body. At the top of the head, the chip was just inserted on top of the brain tissue. The current passed slowly through the tissue.

Sam spoke up. "Do you think that the chip should perhaps have the current pass through it, rather than just lie on top of the huge lump of cerebral tissue?" She explained, "I do not know much about mammalian anatomy, so I am just suggesting that we consider that idea. Whatever is on that microchip, as seen from the symbols, appears to be necessary for the tissue in the head to function."

Quietly she whispered, "Our thinking tissues occur in two parts of an Orthusian body—at the centre of the back and in our head. Maybe it has instructions to start its head tissue functioning, of which we have no information."

Ra spoke up. "If a number of microbes are placed in a liquid culture and a small electric current is passed through the culture, some microbes flow to one end of the electric wire while others move to the other end. The point is that an electric current can stimulate even the smallest living entity, such as a unicell microbe. Maybe one should pass the electric current through one end of the microchip and let it flow through the tissue and reconnect to the other end of the chip. I realize that this is delicate surgical work and there is risk of tissue damage. Ana should be consulted on the risks."

Ana came forward and responded, "Yes, there is a risk of damaging the brain tissue, but our robots are quite skilled at performing this type of microsurgery. The risk may lie in the extremely small microelectric stimulus; we might have missed minimal responses in the respiration of the young cells. I would suggest the smallest be used, then studied for any micro-physiological change after the connection is made. It is possible that there is a need to adapt to the stimuli, and the life form will eventually make the unconscious selection for its survival."

The molecular team decided on the parameters and reprogrammed the robots on what had to be done. The team stressed the use of an ultraminiscule current to begin with. Chuck and his team waited with the full committee, watching from behind closed transparent walls high above. View of the culture tanks was closed off while robots worked in the dark under ultraviolet light.

The watchers decided to return after twenty-four hours, when the process should have been completed. The tired teams retreated to their dorms in the meantime. It was up to the molecular biology teams to work in rotation, regularly checking the in vitro monitors. There were security alarms should any result be out of safety limitations. These teams would call the whole committee to attend should any value drop out of the normal range.

The rooms emptied as the torso in the tanks twirled in its culture fluid with a little gap above the tank. It was quite a sight to see. This naked four-limbed creature was similar to the Orthusians in many ways; it was of a light brown colour but more streamlined, and the appendages were splayed.

The record was reviewed revealing the constant observations over an allotted time period. The upper appendages each had five little attachments, and the lower had the same but built differently. It had black hair on top of its head, under its upper appendages, on its genital region, and between its two lower appendages, and some fine growth on its soft light brown epidermis.

The whole body appeared streamlined to adapt to a fluid environment, as when the whole body twitched, the limbs stretched for a fleeting moment, and the body straightened out into a streamlined board shape. Then, it would curl into a foetal position.

Dia entered uninvited, as she appeared to have the authority to do as she pleased without restrictions. The workers knew that the senior senate committee would be making major decisions, which it would submit as recommendations to the chairman and president of Orthus. People felt that Dia was involved because of the work she and her chosen staff had done in isolating and translating the microdot alien details.

Cleverly, she had arranged the findings as though they were syntax that would form a basic frame for the linguistic computers to recognize. The computers would begin putting forward different abstractions to form a primitive language.

The biodot had found a fit when introduced into the alien life form's constructed molecular tissue. These unusual patterns were transferred to the head organ, as displayed in the diagrams. Dia was present when this all occurred, and it was her idea to do this in the dark with no worker present.

That was two days earlier. Now, she was here and had called the subcommittee to meet her to unveil and re-stimulate the alien using extremely tiny current stimuli. She had her robot record all she said to the workers—in fact, all her conversations. She then instructed the robots to send hard copies to whoever she felt should have them.

This was the first time that scientific workers saw her working. She smiled at all those present and proceeded to ask for their opinions, which were all about the alien in the tank. First, she called on Chuck, the astrophysicist, asking quietly, "As our resident astrophysicist, could you look at the data on the alien and postulate what type of environment needed for its successful existence—more important, list the conditions in which it would not survive?"

Dia, "Please give your report to the robot, who will tabulate it at the end of our search for an adaptive environment. Thank you, Chuck. You need to begin immediately; all your other duties can wait."

She approached Sam, the cosmologist. "Sam, what in the cosmos would restrict such a being from surviving on Orthus? I do not wish to know the obvious. However, can you hypothesize what type of planet would allow optimal growth and survival of its race? Just postulate, invent, and make suggestions as broad as you can. Extract from our little knowledge, but use our library computers to search out and predict. Again, please pass all comments to the robot for assimilation and later abstraction."

Dia continued sharing her abstract requirements with Ra, the microbiologist, with distinctive questions. "Ra, is it true that the extraction of trace elements necessary for good health exists in this alien's digestive system? Do we Orthusians have the same requirement? How similar are our microbiomes and the functions they occupy in good health?"

Ra loudly interrupted, saying, "Look, Dia, all those questions are simple enough and can be answered in your library. You do not need to drag me away from my tasks on this personal investigation you appear to be carrying out."

This firm interruption caught Dia off guard. Before she could respond, Ra continued. "We also have microbial flora in our gut, in our respiratory tract, and on our skin surfaces. This has all been identified, and we have noted the quantities required for optimal health. Second, do we share the same microbiota? Of course not; he subsists on a different diet. We are currently trying to construct what is necessary for his health."

He turned away and then added, "Some elements do not have the same molecular structure. While similar trace elements are essential for his health, they are of a different molecular structure. As a result, he is unable to absorb them. I am working with the physiological biochemists on the details of making these products with a levorotary molecular structure without losing their nutritive value. The geneticists and my group are collaborating in modifying microorganisms to produce the alien's gut flora. The purpose is to extract essential nutritive products as only microorganisms can do efficiently."

"Enough, Ra!" Dia used both verbal and mental telepathy to stop the microbiologist in his tracks; such was her power. "You have explained all well to me. So what is it that we should know about this alien from a microbial perspective? For example, could his bowel flora—should it escape into our environment—cause an epidemic? Is it invasive and pathological, causing us potentially incurable infections? Will we have to develop chemical medicines to keep these potential infections under control?"

Ra looked down at his feet, then quietly said, "Dia, you have no idea how all these scenarios foment my imagination and plague my mind constantly. But it is only I and a small team that cannot be expected do all that is necessary to prevent those scenarios that you have asked to keep from happening. I am becoming quite tired and full of despair. I love this project, and it was an honour to be chosen for this committee. However, this is no longer a challenge but a very tedious affair—" Ra paused suddenly.

He added, "An alien has travelled across the great cosmos to find another life form with which to communicate. Its race must be as lonely or inquisitive as our ancestors were when they set out to find other life forms in our quadrant of the universe many aeons ago. This is what the great cosmos created, as it did with us and our planet."

Abruptly Ra stopped then with passion, "To find another race of its creation is to touch the hand of a Divine Creator. This alien will be our teacher, our future knowledge developer, our stimulus to further our knowledge to unlimited horizons. There is no doubt in my mind that it has come to move us to another dimension far superior to where we are now."

Strangely, Dia didn't try to stop him from speaking. Ra gulped with emotion just to see what he had done with Orthusians' thinking. "If, as our academics postulated, we cannot exist without these microorganisms, then they may be the development of life as we know it. They 'created' us to keep their colonies close together, and to do so, they needed a warm, moist place with conditions necessary for their survival. So they produced what we mammals required to be healthy."

He smiled and looked at all present, "They broke down food material to supply our bodies with essential growth factors that we could not extract using our digestive enzymes Microbes can do that for millions of elements in the cosmos. These unicellular life forms extracted what we needed so we would survive and thus provide the conditions for their own survival."

Ra bent his head down and began to sob. He heard a quiet, relaxed, accented voice enter his head. "I am here not to cause harm but to relive my life on your planet. I have come from afar." Ra fell down unconscious before Dia. She stood back as robot health workers quickly arrived and took him away.

16
CHAPTER

THE ALIEN AWAKENS

Dia followed the robot taking Ra's body to an isolation room while the other scientists on the subcommittee went about their business. An Orthusian physician arrived and gave the robot instructions on how to wake this otherwise-healthy lab scientist. The preliminary scan revealed that Ra was physically exhausted and mentally tired. While it was highly unusual for any Orthusian to drive himself to such extreme exhaustion. This was an unusual project that caused a high degree of physical and mental stress.

With an infusion of fluid and a slight electric shock, Ra opened his eyes and tried to sit up, only to be gently pushed back into a prostrate position on the narrow gurney. He tried to focus, and when his eyes cleared, he saw Dia's blue eyes, most unusual, staring gently down close to his face. The physician stood next to her and began a physical check, which was not routine, since the robots had already done so. Ra was infused with an energy-stimulating fluid. Dia went just out of Ra's sight.

The physician returned to Ra and quietly said, "Ra, microbiologist member of the alien subcommittee, you have deliberately put undue mental and physical stress on your body. Did the committee leader demand this, or was it all your idea of commitment?"

Ra gently sat up. He slowly threw his legs over the edge of the gurney. "Physician, no one forced me to do anything I did not wish to do. I wanted to be on this project to bring back the alien using its tissue cells. Our molecular biologists have been extremely diligent in their tasks after having experienced the return of many of our prehistoric animals and plant species that were once extinct."

Ra looked directly at Dia before adding, "I am all right now and will take rest so this will not happen again."

The physician came closer, looking deep into Ra's eyes as if to search his brain. Ra could feel the nerves in his head being pushed around and probed, searching for abnormalities in the neural synapses. The physician felt a slight weakness in the telepathic sector of Ra's brain but put it down to weariness.

With a sudden jolt, the physician moved away and looked directly at Dia. "It is now your responsibility to keep a close watch on Ra. He has let his telepathic neural structure down to allow only one being to enter and it is not an Orthusian. I saw it, but it is not my task to go any further. He must be delicately handled from now on. Do you understand that his willingness to open up so totally makes him vulnerable? You must do this; no one else has the strength to cope with this syndrome."

With this terse comment, the physician turned and disappeared out of the room and the building. Dia sent the robots away, although one medical robot remained just outside the door. She saw it but knew that this was protocol and said nothing. Ra seemed quiet and calm and looked up at Dia with a smile on his face, an unusual thing for an Orthusian.

AN ASIDE: Orthusians did not smile or laugh even though they could. At one time, all Orthusians smiled after happy occasions but as they had grown and become more educated, they seemed to have completely lost this facial expression, even as newborns. Gentleness remained on their faces as they beheld newborns given to them to raise nourish and be brought up be educated.

Dia came over and sat next to Ra, who shifted away, for sitting this close was an uncomfortable sensation. She looked down as she spoke to him with a gentleness he had never heard, seen, or felt from anyone. He immediately lost his discomfiture with this unusual change in one of the most powerful and feared individuals on the planet. But here she was, sitting close to him, she an older superior with great power that came from her unusual race as seen by her dedication to work.

It was known that she demanded vital unlimited resources from the senior senate committee. She had used her wealth and the planet's resources to reassemble and centralize the library and museums in one portfolio that she designed. Soon, the whole Orthusian education system had set its prospectus based on the powerful knowledge accumulated in her library.

She gently whispered, "Ra, the reason I ask individuals to provide information on their specialty skills and education is because I have been asked to take charge of our alien ambassador's welfare. Such are my demands—that the best biological scientists and medical technologies must be brought into service as befits the alien. This means keeping our visitor in an environment that is secure and that nurtures its health. I thought I heard a strange communication enter your telepathic mind just before you passed out. Do you recall who it was or know of anything that might indicate which individual was contacting you?"

Ra looked directly into Dia's eyes and with a simple, puzzled look and replied, "I do not understand your question. I felt weak, and my mind was very tired, so I gave in and fainted."

Dia, again with her direct, now-piercing look, replied, "You should know that you were one of the first ones I chose to be on this planetary design committee. I will choose the others directly. However, the cosmologists will only be used when we have information from the alien.

All I need are the first few words, syllables, or symbols directly from this life form. I shall use the great power of the library robots to create its language. It is my wish that the alien will assist us in developing the language fully. You will be the alien's partner and companion, if you so desire."

"Well, Dia, that is quite an honour. I am just a simple scientist in a very limited research discipline. What are your reasons for making such an offer to me? I am pleased to have the position, but am I worthy of such a major task? What if I fail? Will you simply discard me? Too much is happening too fast; I need time to rethink my position as a microbiologist and as it pertains to the alien."

Dia stood up and apart as she called the robot to take Ra back to the gurney. "Here is something to think about and maybe perform in your lab. When you have isolated the microbes that are suitable to the alien's good health, take a sample, and put it together with samples from Orthusian gut flora. Observe and document all that happens, and report directly to me. What happens at the microbiome level may have a significant impact on whether we could live with the alien and allow it to freely walk amongst our population."

Ra was surprised at the detail in which the librarian spoke on his subject and how quickly she outlined an experimental design. Dia was indeed a knowledgeable individual, and she seemed to intuitively know that power was the fallout of great information.

BACKGROUND ON DIA:

It was said that Dia was one of the first of her clan, who lived high up in the Orthusian Mountains, to join in the formation of the Orthusian Federation. Her independent clan asked little of the Federation, as the members were completely self-reliant. Their single demand was that they have total freedom to increase their own education and to assist in developing the Orthusian Federation, which would bring all remaining clans under one administration.

Their strong genetic trait was their ability to take in massive amounts of information and mentally organize it in a manner from which it was easy to make deductions. As soon as, there was agreement that use of this skill made them essential to the newly formed Federation of Clans, they had to bring about the accumulation of disparate knowledge from different clans under one administration.

This centralized power was useful to all clans on planet Orthus. Clans would share this pool of knowledge while documents would be prepared for federal committees to allow for such a policy. Hopefully, Federation-developed policies and protocols would bring about a greater understanding of each clan member's requirements to fit into the new Federation.

With such a powerful library of understanding, no race or clan would be left out of the pool of knowledge. Everyone would equally or as needed share the health and welfare benefits, training for outer-space travel, and political positioning. All these fundamental changes had occurred many centuries earlier, but many had never taken Dia's age into consideration.

Ra went back to his laboratory and brought in his bench robots for reprogramming, during which he placed the experimental design into their memory banks. In doing so, he designed the new or revised software so the robots could go about gathering all the knowledge they needed over time while working under renewed safety protocols. He and his robot technicians went about secretly beginning the new processes.

However, the robots would never begin any experiment without first transmitting the idea of the pathway they intended to follow through Ra.

Ra moved into his quarters and immediately fell asleep. He had read the molecular biology report that a mixture of genetically modified microbes was introduced into the alien's gut. The molecular techs had input probes to measure growth success. Respiration as energy had been extracted from the food source before being absorbed. The mixture of gases appeared to be working; it included 78.084 per cent N_2, 20.95 per cent O_2, 0.000053 per cent H_2, and a few inert gases like CO_2.

In fact, the molecular biologists had found a trend in respiration as the gases were introduced to in vitro tissue cultures. That was how they knew the exact amounts of gases necessary for the alien to respire healthily.

Ra got out of his bed in the night but did not seem awake in the darkness. An unseen robot took notice but did not intervene. Ra walked through the darkened hallways and seemed able to avoid the detection systems, which all went into rest mode at a set time. This protected structure used for working on the alien project posed no risk to anyone. The active security detectors were stationed outside the buildings. But there was a silent follower, a miniature robot that kept out of sight while recording all that was happening.

Ra entered the darkened room with the ultraviolet rays on and went up to the tank in which the alien life form was floating. He reached up and turned off the ultraviolet lamps. Pale white light lit up the tank. Ra watched without seeing or understanding.

The alien's eyes opened, and it waved its upper-right-appendage digit to Ra, who was very close to the tank. The alien looked deep into the scientist's open but unseeing eyes. Ra was a giant looking down on a small animal that was built like an Orthusian but brown skinned, rather than green or pink. It closed its eyes and kept close to Ra on the other side of the tank. Ra inhaled deeply, then placed a small keyboard into the tank to provide light. The alien went to the keyboard of lights and stared at it.

It slowly moved its head from right to left, then placed one digit of its small upper appendage on the screen as if to draw, but nothing happened. It turned to Ra, who was still in a comatose state, and pointed to the screen as it repeatedly passed the digit across the lit screen.

Ra turned around and left the tanks without turning on the UV light. He walked back to his sleeping room and went to bed. He did not wake up after the required eight hours of sleep.

When he did get up, he had to rush to meet with his colleagues, whom he found standing in a group, chattering enthusiastically. He pushed his way through to the front, near the dark room where the alien was located. He opened the transparent window, and it was dark with no blue light on. He adjusted the light to white light. The conversation stopped as all eyes turned to watch his activity.

Chuck called out loudly, "Ra, what are you doing? That work should be done by the molecular scientist leader, Ana."

DARRYL GOPAUL

Ra looked over his shoulder and quietly spoke. "I thought we were a team, working on a major project. I come in late, and I find you all gathered, chattering away. What has happened to you all? Where is the leadership here, eh?"

Ra's terse response took Chuck aback; it had a bite in it very unlike that of the scientist who used to be polite and join in on projects with enthusiasm. "Are you feeling unwell, Ra? What is all this show of intolerance about? Are you upset that Dia did not call you up?" Chuck responded.

"I do not know what you are talking about," Ra replied as he slightly adjusted the gas mixture. He moved his hands to where the electric charge should be adjusted when he heard a shrill cry.

"Stop!" shouted Ana. Ra stood back and looked as the whole group stood in shock. "Ra, why are you interfering with the alien life signs without committee discussion and approval? Keep away!" she barked.

The group of scientists seemed on edge. Maga, who remained silent throughout the riled discussion, came and touched Ra on the shoulder. He flinched, as this was an unusual thing for Orthusians to do to each other. "Ra, did Dia invite you to join the maintenance and security committee?"

He looked around before whispering, "She did mention something about needing me, but I got angry with her and refused to follow anything she said. No! I did not agree to join any committee that will look after the alien. Why do you ask?"

Chuck said, "Dia has chosen those she wants with her as the select few to look after the alien. She was willing to give up her precious library, but the senate could not find anyone with the skills required to be trusted with such an important portfolio."

"We do not know for sure, but we think it was a trade-off that she would be given this portfolio, about which she feels very strongly. The condition was that she would choose a group of trusted scientists to work with her," replied Sam.

17
CHAPTER

WITHER THE CHOSEN

Ra laughed loudly. The laugh of an Orthusian is like the howl of a wild dog or a lonely wolf. "Dia has chosen, and that is why you are all excited; you wish to be chosen."

Ra walked around them and then looked at the floating alien. "Ana, it is time to remove the ultraviolet light from the tank. If there were infected microbes in the tanks, your tissue culture would have been ruined. Your monitoring system would have detected the presence of microbes, and the tissue would not have shown signs of health. Furthermore, the ultraviolet light might harm the delicate superficial organs of this alien."

Ana, red cheeked and obviously aroused, screamed, "How dare you tell me about my profession! My skills and those of my workers brought this physical being back into existence from a few cells. It was Chuck's team that unravelled the microchip that had imprints inserted into the being's brain cavity. How dare a microbiologist and an astrobiologist imply—"

"Stop! What is wrong with all of you?" Ra exclaimed, interrupting. "A team effort where no one group is any better than another is what has brought the alien to this state. But when are we going to take the next step, which is to bring our visitor to life, when it can begin to train us in its language?

"Yes, you have done a good job, but do not allow your slavish following of set protocols damage the alien's delicate tissues," Ra stated. "What does UV light do? It kills microbes, and what can happen if you leave it on indefinitely? You do not know, do you?" he asked. "You see, Dia asked that I compare the alien's microbiome with ours. With a few modifications, its microbiome reacts the same way as ours."

Ra stopped and looked at everyone else as a group of new graduates doing their training rounds with him. "Your lesson for today's committee members: 'Microbes, unicellular entities, fill the cosmos as the only viable life form in the midst of severe types of toxic radiation and other physical dangers in the cosmos. Even with extreme heat and cold, little-to-no atmosphere, and limited moisture, these microscopic entities were and are the only life forms that our returning travellers have brought back from outer space. I have the complete collection. My stock of these unicellular microscopic life forms may be the key to the development of all life in the cosmos." He looked at the team as new recruits moving his eyes from one to the other.

Ra lectured, "These microscopic life forms have shown they can survive in spite of all that the great cosmos throws at them, and when conditions are favourable to them, they vegetate and become living entities that reproduce. They are endowed to do a single task, and they do it very efficiently. It is in their genome, where billions of inducible enzymes are used to break cosmic substrates into their elemental parts. They also do so wherever there is a barrier to their survival."

As he finished his diatribe, Ana shouted and pointed "The alien moved. It stretched out, standing in the fluid on its two lower appendages, just as Orthusians did, with its head out of the fluid. It reached out for the computer screen that Ra had provided under his night walk and touched it. Nothing happened, but Ra went to the major keyboard and typed in "Sensitive screen."

Head turned away, the alien placed a digit on the screen and moved the digit in a downward streak. The lights wrote, "Ra." The alien turned around to face the group through the thick glass. Then using one digit, it came to the glass and opened its hollow black eyes. It pointed to Ra, who was close. It beckoned him to come forward, and it moved forward quickly. It pointed to its head and then spoke what sounded like computer language.

Ra pointed to his chest and said, "I am Ra." The alien closed its eyes, then pointed to its head, then tapped its head. Ra closed his own eyes and let a telepathic voice enter his head. Ra spoke telepathically to the being. "Go to the screen and show." He opened his eyes to see the alien looking at him. He pointed to the internal screen and mimicked the drawing with one of his digits.

The alien moved to the screen and with one finger drew symbols: *A, B, C, D, E, F = bed*. With that, it put its hands together, closed its eyes, and then floated in a sleeping position.

"Ah! Just what I thought; it is ready to communicate. Move over, Ra. Rather, stand next to me, and let my robots go through the exercise," Dia said, entering and taking over.

In a matter of minutes, the alien had a working response with the robots, using symbols. However, all telepathic biopaths were open to the committee members, who closed their eyes to listen to the sing-song voice of their first alien on planet Orthus. Dia brilliantly managed the response and began a strange dialogue, for she created the translation's design as the exchange went on.

The alien had shown its own alphabet with simple examples and symbols that it could physically display. The self-programmable robots took over as whole sentences in the alien language were shown. This was followed by a dictionary of alien words with their Orthusian translations. The alien became frenetic as it tried to explain that it had a spouse. "Look for more cells in the capsule."

This was all displayed using symbols, and Ana shouted loudly, "I knew there were other capillary tubes of cells! Tell the alien that it should have its spouse soon. I shall have my staff immediately begin working now that we have all the conditions under which we can speed up the process. Dia, please tell everyone that we need unlimited resources. We shall work nonstop until we have the cells of its spouse."

Lesson 1

Dia recorded every word, and she embarked on an intensive study of the alien language. She slowly translated as the alien delighted the secret small group of onlookers with writing. It seemed to mouth words with gestures, which the robot translated for the senate. Then, all of this was allowed to be sent across the whole planet. Into every Orthusian domicile and institution, the following transcript was sent for all to understand.

> My name is Adams. I have a spouse with me. We came from a planet in a small solar system. In our time, it would have been 2030. Our planet was formed around 4.5 billion years ago. Do the mathematics, and see how old my civilization is now.

He drew the solar system from which he came and laid down the coordinates to its location just outside the Milky Way. He showed how time was calculated—what a day was relative to the sun. He drew the sun and the Earth and showed what a night and a day looked like on Earth. He worked tirelessly to describe all he wanted them to understand. He drew the carbon and oxygen atoms, then the nitrogen and hydrogen. He showed the basic linkages of these simple elements. He explained why he needed the mixture of gases to breathe.

In response, the senior senate committee members came to see for themselves this naked alien with seemingly unlimited energy explaining his presence. In response, the Orthusian leadership had every teaching establishment begin teaching the alien's language to all Orthusians, from junior to old. The library robots developed the language and recorded all the alien was showing and saying to them.

Robots produced tanks that would allow the alien, now called by his name of Adams, to move out of his tanks. He wanted a covering for his body, and he showed how he wanted to dress. The robots went in search of artificial materials and made a white sheet, with an opening at the top, to cover his body.

He wanted privacy for his toilet, and that was also provided. He needed pure, clean water to drink and with which to bathe his body. His food had improved, but he signalled the formula for carbohydrates, protein, and lipids as part of his diet. The alien went to sleep after this open display. The alien had selected Ra for the intensive part of his awakening. The other team members referred the alien's wishes to the robots.

Afterwards, whatever that the alien Adams received had to first be tested for safety and for toxic effects. The alien cells were used for in vivo testing under stringent conditions, as Ana and her dedicated team of workers laid down. Chuck worked tirelessly with his lab team in fulfilling the robotic requirements in defined tasks. He had a special group whose sole function was to monitor the robots' maintenance and security from external tampering on a continuous roster.

Lesson 2

Adams spoke to the group but focused on Ra and Dia. "My spouse cannot use my brain scans, for they were done after she died. We planned this adventure together, but I did not have all her brain tracings; I remember, for these were my last memory tracings. Both of us agreed to keep our genetic tissues from our bone marrow and send them in the capsule. She does not have a record of my last days, only the last days before her death. I shall share my tracings with her, and maybe she will remember her past with me. Just bring her back, for we planned this adventure throughout our lifetimes on Earth, our home planet."

The library robots were in full recording and analysing mode as they generated millions of pieces of documents with every word Adams said. He turned around and began to explain that he was a teacher at a university of higher learning. He was also a scientist, like Ra, and his spouse was a scientist, more like Ana, but she diagnosed blood diseases caused by genetic fault.

Dia had opened the door to alien Adams, and the by-product of her position was any request that teacher Adams made was to be granted. A number of robots were involved in logging everything he did or said, and after Dia's screening, they transferred the information to the senior senate committee, which then passed it on to the public at large. Adams had been seen on the planet's national screens speaking in his strange language, which was translated for everyone.

After a few months, he was ushered into a quiet room, away from the public and committee members, to see his spouse floating in a tank similar to what he had been in just a short time ago. Adams did not show any special feelings of joy but stared at the being similar to himself. He looked up at Ana and her team and asked, "When will you wake her up?"

Ana replied, "She should be awake. We implanted brain tracings from her genetic material but have held back from implanting yours until she asks that it be done. There has been no response even though the autonomic sensual and neural patterns appear to be functioning. She is a different colour; she is white, not like you, brown."

Adams spoke up. "Give her time, and I will use little shocks in the interim. Leave me to wake her in the dark. Just one thing—you know how I asked that you make tea for me? Can I have a cup now? I also want everyone to leave me, including the robots. Please leave us alone. There should be no documenting systems working when we are together."

The blinds were drawn and the lights lowered, and Adams was left in the dark. Soon, a steaming-hot cup of tea arrived by robot. The robot handed the cup to him, and he was left alone. Adams leaned over the tank as the body floated near the surface head first. He looked at the closed eyes and pale brown hair. "Eve," he whispered, "I have a cup of your favourite tea. I taught the Orthusians how to dry the tea leaves, and soon, they knew how to make tea. They are drinking tea now and loving it. Wake up, sweetie. We are here in the future, just as we planned. It is time for you to wake up."

The body floated up, and there was a gulping noise as fluid was expelled from the lungs. Adams stepped back, for he did not remember how he had got out of the tank. After the gulping and expelling of fluid, she had a great intake of air. Then, the eyes opened. They were dark holes with no coloured irises. Then a husky voice spoke. "Adam, I am never going to open my eyes while they are around. Give me the tea."

He handed it over. "Why don't you come out and join me?" Adams asked. "They are very clever. They followed my directions in bringing us back. Come out and join me. It is safe here."

She said, "Are you nuts, Adam! Can you not see what is happening? What is wrong with you? We need to return to Earth, to our families—at least be buried where they can come visit our graves."

Adams loudly responded, "Eve, these are great folks. We cannot go back. We were recreated from our cells and our brain tracings. On Earth, we died. We never wanted to go into the ground, anyway; we wanted to be cremated and have our ashes sent into the natural forests. Why are you so afraid?"

In fear, she responded, "Adam, look around you. These are not humanoids; they are lizards. They are making us so they can eat us later and probably make farms where they can make a ready supply of fresh human meat in their labs, just clones of our bodies. They will soon get hungry, and they will attack us. I do not intend to live on a planet that is overrun by creepy lizards!"

End.

AFTERWORD

After man's evolution from the trees he kept close to his tribe and built a social community. The history of man is filled with conjecture of what happens after death. Towards this end, many civilizations throughout human history have constructed edifices to try to return to this preworld or to travel to a more fitting paradise.

Certain religious philosophies teach that humans will return to this physical world through reincarnation. They will return in a variety of life forms; that does not necessitate human form. Others postulate a distinct spirituality from a creationist fact of a soul returning, or that the immortal part of humankind is indestructible; it will return in human form.

In this story, a modern twist plays out in sending the departed' ashes and a piece of their tissue into deep space. These are the remains of a science-fiction writer and his spouse of sixty-plus years. On a planet on the other side of the galaxy, the capsule, and its contents, is found billions of light years later by a highly evolved alien society. Bringing their best scientists together, the aliens use the tissues to bring back the whole beings.

Adams and his wife, Eve, return to find their naked selves in a tissue-culture tank. The story uses all the current stages of laboratory stem-cell research and tissue-culture growth in returning a being from a single cell.

Why does the deceased author wish to participate in this celestial experiment, and why does he need his spouse with him? Does he feel that there are other, more developed life forms in the cosmos? As a scientist, he intuitively knows that in one human lifetime, he could never find such a cosmic being; thus, he gives himself the time of eternity.

When his own planet had long since disappeared into a supernova, he is brought back into an alien world, and his new journey begins.

OTHER BOOKS AND SHORT STORIES BY DARRYL GOPAUL

Published Books

- *Bacteria: The Good, the Bad, the Ugly*
- *Tales of Myths and Fantasy*
- *Around the World on Three Underwear*
- *Six Decades to Wisdom … (Maybe)*
- *Sonnets of a Human Soul—A Book of Poems*
- *A Collection of Fables and Tales*
- *Diagnosis*
- *Adventures in the Cosmos*
- *Imaginary Epics from the Cosmos*
- *A Science Fiction Trilogy from the Novel* Escape from Jipadara
  - *Evolution*
  - *Tribulations*
  - *Revelations*

- *Encyclopaedia Library*
- *Biological Key*
- *A Lyrical Biography and a Gastronomic Vacation*
- *Stories Clouded in Mystery (Once Upon a Time)*
- *Caravan Boy*
- *Glossary of Poems*

Upcoming Books – Manuscripts in its unedited form are ready but it takes time and money to bring them into text for novels

- *Alien Manuscripts, Onyx Cubes, and Runes*
- *One Day in a Life (Prague Diaries)*
- *Against the Implementation of Healthcare Reform in Canada*

Short Stories *(Created for TV and small independent movies)*

- "From Trinidad Tales of Myths and Fantasy"
- "Aunt Lucy Saw the Devil"
- "Do Not Mess with the Devil's Handbook"
- "Hello! I Am Back (from the Dead of Course)"
- "La Diablesse, Soucouyant and Bois Bandy"

Science-Fiction Books

- *Space Academy*
- *Proto*
- *Strange Encounter—Parallel Dimension*

Other

- *The Request*
- *Oakridge Fen*
- *Immunologist*
- *Chasing after My Shade*
- *The Golden Infidel*

- *Soliloquy*
- *Luiz's Odyssey*
- *There Is a Duck on My Roof*
- *Guru Ramesh*

Printed in the United States
By Bookmasters